LOVE BLOOMS

LOVE BLOOMS

•

Eva Swain

AVALON BOOKS
NEW YORK

Published by Thomas Bouregy & Co., Inc.
160 Madison Avenue, New York, NY 10016

Library of Congress Cataloging-in-Publication Data

Swain, Eva, 1948–
    Love blooms / Eva Swain.
        p. cm.
    ISBN 978-0-8034-9933-1 (acid-free paper)
    1. Divorced mothers—Fiction.   I. Title.
    PS3619.W346L68 2009
    813'.6—dc22

                                            2008031389

PRINTED IN THE UNITED STATES OF AMERICA
ON ACID-FREE PAPER
BY HADDON CRAFTSMEN, BLOOMSBURG, PENNSYLVANIA

For Dave, always

Chapter One

Marcie Connor wasn't sure what made her wake up. Something had disturbed her sleep, and once she was awake, she heard her dogs barking and a vehicle outside the house. She could see no car lights from her bedroom windows, which was odd. If someone had rolled up the driveway, the headlights would have flashed across her windows.

She looked at the clock, realizing it was almost 2:00 A.M. She could still hear the vehicle, but the sound came from the wrong direction for it to be in the driveway. She got out of bed and went to the windows. Her bedroom was on the second floor of the house, with views of the driveway from both the front and side.

The lights on in the yard did not reveal any cars

1

other than those belonging to her and her great-aunt. She couldn't see the intrusive vehicle, but she could hear it. Its engine was being revved over and over.

Marcie realized that if the vehicle wasn't in the driveway, it could only be in one of the fields. She reached for the clothes she had dropped into the hamper the night before. Quickly pulling on a pair of jeans and a T-shirt, she went out into the hallway.

Her Great-aunt Jane, who lived with Marcie and her three children, came out of her room at the other end of the hall.

Flipping on a light switch, Marcie saw the distress on the older woman's face.

"Call the sheriff's office, Aunt Jane. Someone is driving through the fields. I'm going out to see who it is."

Jane Southerland admonished Marcie to be careful and went down the stairs to make the call. The farm was outside the city limits, and they depended on the county sheriff if they needed help.

Marcie grabbed a flashlight from the hall table, flipped on all the outside light switches, flooding the yard with illumination, and ran outside. She told the dogs in the pen behind the house to hush, then ran toward the sound of the vehicle, outraged to see it in one of the daylily fields.

The dirty white pickup truck with an orange

dragon emblazoned on the side was circling around and around in the middle of the daylilies, and Marcie stumbled to a halt as she saw the damage it had done to the acres of plants. Deep ruts left by its massive tires scored the soft ground, and the remains of daylily plants lay crushed and scattered across the formerly tidy field.

Marcie saw three people in the truck, getting a good look at the passenger nearest the right-hand door. He saw her coming across the yard and yelled something to the driver, who spun the steering wheel and took off across the field, heading toward the driveway. The truck bogged down in the soft dirt, and the driver revved the engine, trying to get it moving.

For a moment the truck remained stuck, and the driver quickly shifted into reverse and then into a forward gear, rocking the pickup until it took off again. The windshield was almost completely covered with mud thrown up from the field, and Marcie wondered how the driver could see anything through it.

As the truck broke loose, a fountain of mud flew up behind it, and the pickup roared off into the night, bouncing across the ruts and out onto the driveway. The passenger stared back at Marcie, and she knew she would not forget his youthful face or his bizarre haircut.

She was able to use the flashlight to get some of

the license-plate numbers and letters, and she began saying them over and over so she wouldn't forget them. She ran back to the house to find a pen and paper so she could write them down.

As Marcie stood just inside the door, jotting a description of the truck and the passenger she had gotten a look at, Aunt Jane came down the stairs.

"The sheriff's office said they're pretty busy. There are two auto accidents they're working, with serious injuries at both crash scenes. Is there a lot of damage to the daylilies?"

"I don't know, Aunt Jane." Marcie dreaded telling her aunt just how much damage she had seen. "I didn't get a good look. I got part of the license plate, and I wanted to write it down before I forgot it. I'm going back out now to check the damage. The truck was in the west field, where the new introductions are. We won't be able to see the full extent of the damage until it gets light."

As Marcie turned to go back outside, a voice from the top of the stairs stopped her.

"Mom, what's going on? Why are you and Aunt Jane up? Why were the dogs barking?"

Marcie looked up to see her seven-year-old daughter, Emily, at the top of the stairs.

"Everything's okay. There was a truck driving around in the yard, but it's gone now. You head back to bed. Aunt Jane and I are going to go outside to look around. Did your brother and sister wake up?"

Emily yawned sleepily. "No, Mom, they're still sleeping." She started down the steps toward her mother.

Marcie went up the stairs and took her daughter by the hands. "You go back to bed now, sweetheart." She kissed and hugged her daughter and watched as she went back to her room.

When she and Jane went outside, Jane took a deep breath. She laid a hand on Marcie's arm. "Emily will find out soon enough that there was some trouble here tonight."

"I know, Aunt Jane, but I want to keep her from worrying as much as possible. She's turned so serious since her father and I divorced."

As the two women got farther from the house, their flashlights revealed the damage done by the joyriding teenagers.

Marcie felt sick as she took in the ruined field. It had rained steadily for two days, and the earth in the fields was soft and soggy. That meant that the damage would be worse than just the fact that the plants were shredded and crushed. Their tender roots were likely also destroyed, perhaps making the daylily crop in this field a total loss.

Only a close inspection in daylight would tell the whole story. The two women stood silently for a moment, surveying the vandalism. Then Marcie heard her great-aunt sob.

Marcie quickly put her arms around the older

woman, leading her away from the ruined plants. They walked back to the house, and Marcie put the flashlights back into a drawer in the hall table. She led Jane into the kitchen and flipped on the light. Jane sat at the kitchen table, and Marcie realized she had never seen her great-aunt look so tired and old. She put water on to boil for tea and got cups and tea bags from a cabinet.

"Why would anyone do this? If this is someone's idea of a joke, it certainly isn't funny. I hope the sheriff catches them quickly." Jane looked up at Marcie. "How could someone just destroy a person's work like that? What could they have been thinking?"

Marcie and her parents sold perennials such as irises, daylilies, hostas, ornamental grasses, and peonies. They also grew and sold berries, which were available on a pick-your-own basis or already boxed during berry season.

The plants were sold to visitors who came to the farm from all over the country, as well as over the Internet. Marcie and her brother, Jack, had set up the Web site and online catalog. The family dug and shipped the roots and rhizomes to their customers at the proper planting times, depending on where the customers lived.

Growing and selling the plants and berries was definitely a labor of love. The farm had been in the family for several generations, and there had always been family members to plant and tend the flowers they loved. Marcie's grandfather, Jack Greer, had been the first to go into the nursery business full-time. Marcie's father had inherited both his father's farm and his love of horticulture.

Marcie's brother, Jack, and his wife, Nancy, raised quarter horses and border collies on the farm. Jack had never shown the same love of raising plants that Marcie and her parents shared. He had worked full-time when needed, but he had also been happy to have Marcie move back to the farm after her divorce, as it had allowed him to get back to doing what he really loved to do. Jack and Nancy Greer's horses and dogs were prize-winning champions, and Jack was well-known in his own right.

Marcie loved every aspect of the work on Harmony Farm, and the years she had spent away from it at college and in her short marriage were the saddest of her life. Returning to the farm after her divorce, Marcie had stepped back into the family business as if she'd never been away.

The peace and tranquility of life on the farm had been a balm to her heart and soul after her disastrous marriage. Being the divorced mother of three children at age twenty-eight certainly hadn't ever been part of her plans, but having a job and a home to come back to had made things easier.

Shortly after Marcie had returned, her mother's aunt, Jane Southerland, had fallen and broken her arm. Jane's oldest daughter had wanted Jane to move into a retirement home, but Marcie and her mother, Sharon Greer, knowing Jane's fierce independence, had invited her to live at Harmony Farm. She'd accepted their invitation gladly and moved in with Marcie to help her with her three children, leaving Marcie more time to work with her parents.

"I'm sure they weren't thinking much, Aunt Jane. Maybe they'd been drinking. We'll find out when they're caught." Marcie poured the boiling water into the teacups. "I've never seen that truck around the area before. It may not have been anyone local driving. I can't imagine anyone who lives around here getting involved in something like this, but if they were drinking, I suppose it's possible."

The farm was well-known locally, and Marcie hoped no one she knew had been responsible for the damage. She had only seen the one boy's face and hadn't seen the driver or the other passenger, so she had no way of knowing if they were area teens.

They drank their tea in silence. When Marcie looked at the kitchen clock, she realized it was almost four-thirty in the morning.

"It's too late for me to go back to bed now. Why don't you go back to bed for a while, though, and try to rest? I can do some work in the office until it gets light enough to go outside and survey the damage." Marcie rinsed the cups and put them on the counter next to the sink.

She hugged Jane and watched as the older woman walked slowly up the steps. Then she went upstairs and checked on her daughter, who had fallen asleep again. It was so hard to believe that anyone would deliberately destroy years of work for a few minutes of joyriding.

The plants in that particular field had not been available for sale this season but would have been offered next year.

Once Marcie's father decided which new introductions were ready to be sold commercially, the plants were sectioned into their own areas of the fields. It was a painstaking process, hybridizing and growing the seedlings, but to Marcie it was magical.

Marcie pushed the thought of the destroyed plants out of her mind and went into the office. She sat at her desk and logged on to her computer. She and her parents kept detailed records of everything they grew.

They had to know every last detail about their plants in order to assure their customers they were getting precisely what they wanted. They had records that dated back to the early days of her grandfather's breeding program. She was thankful that whoever had done this awful thing had waited until after they were through delivering the plants for this year. If the damage had occurred during the busy delivery season, or in any field but that one, the financial loss would have been much greater.

She pulled up a map of the daylily field, noting which plants were growing there. They had only seen the damage to that one field, but it was possible there was vandalism in other fields as well. She would have to wait for daylight to be able to inspect the rest of the farm. She hoped the damage was confined to the one field.

As she stared at the glowing computer screen, Marcie heard a noise behind her. She swung around in her chair to see Emily enter the office. Wearing her favorite pink pajamas and fluffy pink slippers, Emily climbed up onto her mother's lap.

"Hey, Emily. Why aren't you in bed? I peeked in on you earlier, and you were sleeping." Marcie pulled her daughter close, feeling the girl's body tremble.

"I woke up again," Emily whispered. "I'm scared to go back to bed."

Marcie hugged her tightly. "I'm sorry, sweetie. Why don't you stay here with me for a while?"

Her daughter nestled in her lap, and Marcie smoothed Emily's hair and kissed the top of her head. She felt her daughter begin to relax. Emily lay her head against Marcie's shoulder, and Marcie began to rub her back gently.

"I tried to go back to sleep—honest, Mom. Will Grandma and Grandpa be really mad at us?"

Marcie kissed her daughter's cheek. "No, sweetie, I promise they won't be mad at us."

"They won't yell at us like Daddy used to?" Emily looked into her mother's face.

"I promise they won't yell at us. When I was a little girl, about your age, your grandfather and grandmother never yelled at me. Even when I didn't behave or do all my chores, they never yelled. They will know that what happened wasn't our fault. They'll be sad because of the damage to the plants, but they won't be mad at us."

Marcie pulled Emily against her. Tears stung her eyes as she thought about the ugly scenes her daughter had witnessed between Marcie and her ex-husband, Jim Connor. There had been far too many of them during their short marriage.

It wasn't long before Marcie felt her daughter relax against her, and she realized that Emily had fallen asleep. She printed the pages she was working on, turned off the computer, and leaned back in her chair, cuddling her daughter closely. She carried the girl upstairs, settling her into bed without waking her.

Marcie went back downstairs to the kitchen. Emily's question had brought back memories Marcie tried hard to suppress, memories of her ex-husband and the angry words he had frequently hurled at her. He had often been angry and belligerent even when sober, blaming others for his shortcomings and failures. Marcie had been his favorite target. He was physically abusive when drunk, which had happened more and more often toward the end of their short-lived marriage.

Having been raised to always try to do her best, to make the best of every situation, and to get along with others, Marcie was an easy target for the sadistic tendencies that drinking brought out in her ex-husband. She had tried to live up to her Christian principles, and the very fact that she could had infuriated Jim and made him even more abusive.

She had been pregnant with the twins for only a few months when he left, so they had never known their father. He hadn't wanted more children after Emily and had often accused Marcie of letting herself get pregnant again in order to spite him. He had refused to believe it was possible for birth-control pills to fail, and when they had found out she was expecting twins, he had gone so far as to accuse her of being unfaithful to him. Citing the fact that there weren't any twins in either of their families, he had refused to believe she was carrying his babies.

He had become enraged and had struck her across the face for the first time. Usually when he'd wanted to punish her for some perceived slight on her part, he'd left bruises in places that didn't show. She had often hidden the bruises through her choice of clothing. But this was the limit.

She had tried so hard to please him before she realized she would never be able to do so and she had gone to see a lawyer about a divorce. Jim had saved her the trouble by leaving of his own accord. Shortly after he left, *he* had filed for divorce, and Marcie had been only too happy to let him have an uncontested divorce.

She and the children hadn't seen or heard from him since the day he'd walked out of the house.

It had been hard to reconcile the charming man Jim Connor had been before their marriage to the ill-tempered, fault-finding monster he had become so soon after the happy day. Marcie had struggled with feelings of guilt and inadequacy for a long time and had never been able to tell anyone of the relief she had felt when Jim had walked out. She knew that her children should have contact with their father, but she was secretly relieved that they didn't.

Little Emily had been aware of the problems between her parents, had seen her father strike her mother, and Marcie knew that her daughter was affected by the abuse. Marcie had made the decision to divorce Jim because she couldn't bear the thought that her daughter would grow up thinking it was okay for a man to abuse his wife.

She pushed her dark thoughts away, vowing yet again to leave her ex in the past, where he belonged.

Marcie knew that her parents would be upset when she called to tell them of the vandalism on the farm, but they would not be angry with her over something she had had no control over. She hated to interrupt their vacation, but knew she would have to contact them as soon as possible. She also had to let Jack and Nancy know what had happened. Their house was far enough away from Marcie's that they would not have seen the truck drive up into the fields of flowers. Jack's house and barns were secluded on the far side of the property.

The call to her parents went as Marcie expected. They wanted to come home immediately. The Greers were visiting friends in St. Louis, and Marcie had assured her parents that there was no reason to cut their visit short. Nothing could be done until the sheriff sent someone out to survey the damage. She knew her father would come home as soon as possible, though, no matter what she said.

When she phoned Jack, he suggested that he go out driving around to see if he could find the truck with the dragon logo, an idea Marcie vetoed. She convinced him to let the sheriff's department handle the matter.

Late in the afternoon, Marcie realized that the sheriff's office had not contacted her yet. She called to see when they might expect a visit from someone in law enforcement and was told that her call had been logged and that someone would contact her. It wasn't a satisfactory answer, but Marcie knew she would just have to wait for an officer to show up at the farm.

She wanted to start to clean up the field, but she didn't dare do anything until the sheriff sent someone to look at the damage. By the time she put the children to bed that night, she was getting annoyed, because the sheriff had not sent anyone out to the farm. She and Jane had spent the day doing chores outside, cleaning the house, and tending the various animals that called the farm home. The children and the chores had kept them busy, but waiting for someone from the sheriff's office to arrive had kept both of them watching the clock.

As they went upstairs to bed that night, Marcie hugged her great-aunt. "I'm so glad you're here, Aunt Jane. I don't know what the children and I would do without you."

"Nonsense, Marcie. You have given me a home and a sense of being needed and wanted. I'm so glad to be here with you and the children. Besides, I'm not ready for a nursing home yet."

At seventy-two years of age, Jane Southerland was spry, physically fit, and as hard a worker as most people many years younger. Marcie blessed the day that Jane had come to live with her.

Jane stayed home from church on Sunday morning, in case someone from the sheriff's department came to investigate. When Marcie got home from church, she wasn't happy to find out that no one had come by yet.

She called the sheriff's department and was put

through to a deputy. He didn't seem very sympathetic to her problem. When she asked again when someone would be out to assess the damage, she was told that calls were being answered in the order of "priority assigned."

In other words, she thought, *we don't care about your problem.* She spoke to the man for a few minutes and was not satisfied with his answers. She hung up the phone, not really expecting to see anyone from the sheriff's department.

Chapter Two

On Monday, three days after the truck had ruined the daylily field, the sheriff's office still had not sent anyone out to Harmony Farm. Marcie had to go into town to do some errands, and she decided she would stop by the sheriff's office. She knew Ben Jamison, the sheriff, and she planned to sit in his office until she spoke to him personally.

She made printouts of Harmony Farm's overall sales figures and the figures from the season's sale of plants from the ruined field, along with a printout showing the type and number of daylilies that had been planted on the acreage in question. She retrieved a copy of their catalog, which was available by mail, as well as the Internet catalog. She also printed off a few pages of Internet catalogs from other nursery farms, in case anyone thought she was inflating her prices. She knew that people who didn't frequent the farm might have a hard time realizing the value of the plants that had been destroyed, and she wanted to have proof of her claims.

Her father's insurance agent had been to the farm the day after the vandalism had occurred, and he hadn't had any problems recognizing the amount of damage, as he and his wife were longtime customers. Marcie wanted to be sure the sheriff understood just how much of a loss the destroyed plants represented. She hoped that whoever had done the damage could be forced to pay for it, and she needed the sheriff's office to investigate her claim.

She dressed casually in a blue denim skirt and jade green blouse that brought out the color of her eyes. She rarely wore makeup but did slick on a little lip gloss in a rust shade that didn't look too obvious. Black ballet flats, her favorite shoulder bag, and a jade green lightweight jacket completed her outfit. It wasn't dressy, by any means, but it was comfortable. It would do for running errands. Pulling her hair away from her face, she anchored it with rhinestone clips, leaving the ends curling around her neck and shoulders.

The first stop on her list of errands took her to the sheriff's office. Marcie spoke to the desk clerk, asking to speak to Sheriff Jamison, and was told that he was on vacation. Deputy Sheriff Kyle Hughes was in charge. She asked to speak to him and told the clerk the nature of her problem. The clerk picked up the phone and called the deputy's office.

Marcie could hear only one side of the conversation, but it was apparent that Deputy Sheriff Hughes did not want to speak to her. She was growing impatient and couldn't understand why her problem didn't seem important enough to warrant investigation.

When the clerk hung up the phone and informed Marcie that Hughes did not have time to speak to her, Marcie found her impatience turning to anger. She could see the office door marked DEPUTY SHERIFF and realized she was only fifteen feet from the person she needed to speak to.

She took a few deep breaths, trying to calm herself. "Please inform him that I do not plan to leave until I speak to him. This is really important." Marcie spoke quietly but firmly.

The clerk seemed to sense that Marcie was close to losing her temper and tried to smooth things over. Her explanation that the deputy sheriff was busy left Marcie unmoved. She silently vowed to stand by the clerk's desk all day if necessary.

A few minutes later the phone rang, and as the clerk picked it up, Marcie slipped around the desk and ran toward the deputy sheriff's office. Just as she opened the door, the clerk finished her conversation and darted after Marcie.

"Ms. Connor, please wait! You can't just barge in there!"

Kyle Hughes was sitting behind his desk, his thoughts going around and around. He was worried about his nephews. His brother's boys were seventeen and fourteen, and since Tom was away from home so much, the boys seemed to be running wild. His sister-in-law, Janie, didn't seem to be able to control them. Tom Jr., especially, seemed to resent him if he tried to talk to them. As their uncle, and as a deputy sheriff, he was worried that they would get into serious trouble if not reined in soon.

As she opened the door, all Marcie could think about was explaining her problem to the man in charge. She stopped dead as she entered the room, shocked to see that the man she needed to speak to was simply sitting in his chair, staring out the window behind the desk. He had his hands clasped behind his head, his booted feet propped up on the window ledge. He swung around and rose from his chair in one fluid movement just as the clerk crashed into Marcie's back.

Marcie dropped her folder, scattering papers across the office floor. She was staring at the large, angry man confronting her across the desk. Something seemed to crackle in the air, and she suddenly felt as if all the air was being sucked out of her lungs, leaving her unable to draw a breath. She barely heard the clerk speaking to her; the woman's voice seemed to come from far away.

"I'm sorry, Kyle. I tried to tell her you were busy. She ran back here when I answered the phone." She grabbed Marcie's arm and tried to pull her out of the office.

As the woman grasped her arm and pulled, Marcie felt her world come back into focus, and her anger at the arrogant deputy sheriff returned.

She pulled her arm free and turned to look at the man standing behind the desk. Without stopping to think, Marcie asked coldly, "And just what would he be 'busy' doing? Counting clouds?" Heedless of the expression on the deputy's face, or of the clerk, who was still trying to smooth things over, Marcie continued. "I have been waiting three days for someone from this office to come to Harmony Farm to investigate the damage done by vandals, and you're just sitting here staring out the window?"

The clerk spoke before the deputy could. "Look, Ms. Connor, we really don't have time to investigate damage done to a flower garden. Some kid probably drove off the road, ran through your flowers, and drove on again. If there is no real damage, such as to a vehicle or building, it doesn't warrant investigating."

Her tone of voice and emphasis on the word *investigating* left no doubt as to her feelings on the subject of *flower gardens.*

"How much could a few flowers be worth, anyway?" she said.

The deputy still had not spoken, but Marcie saw a smile start to curl his lips. The fact that the lips were on a very handsome face did not escape Marcie's notice. Nor did the fact that his blue eyes looked like chips of frozen sky against the tan of his face. She wondered for a brief moment if his anger was because she had burst into his office or if there was another problem bothering him.

Marcie looked from the deputy to the clerk in disbelief. She felt her cheeks burn as she tried to rein in her temper. She had no way of knowing that, at that moment, with her checks slightly flushed and her green eyes flashing with temper, the deputy was thinking she was the most beautiful woman he had seen outside the movies or television. With her dark auburn hair tumbling down around her shoulders, she looked positively enchanting, making it hard for him to think about the reason she was standing in front of his desk.

Bending to pick up some of the papers she had dropped, she began reading aloud the figures on profits from the spring and summer plant and berry sales. When she gave the total amount, the clerk gasped in disbelief.

"You make that much money selling flowers?"

"Plants, actually. We don't sell flowers. And the field that was damaged covered several acres, with thousands of plants."

The deputy spoke for the first time, his accent making Marcie wonder from where he came. She knew he wasn't from Arkansas as soon as he spoke.

"How do you sell that many plants around here? I wouldn't think there could be room for that many plants in the whole state." His voice was low and resonant, and Marcie liked the sound.

Before Marcie could reply, another voice spoke from the doorway.

"Good morning, Kyle, Sarah. What's been happening since I've been on vacation?"

Marcie and the clerk both turned toward the doorway to see Sheriff Ben Jamison. He smiled when he saw Marcie.

"Marcie Connor, what a pleasant sight for these old eyes. How are you?" He came forward and hugged Marcie. "I haven't seen you in a dog's age, young lady. How are your parents?"

His entrance defused the angry situation, and Marcie smiled as she answered him.

"I'm fine, Sheriff, and so are Mama and Dad. They're in St. Louis, but I'm afraid they're going to have to cut their vacation short, considering what's happened."

Sheriff Jamison looked around at the occupants

of the office, then down at the floor. He bent and picked up one of the papers. The page he picked up was the computer map of the ruined garden. The next thing he picked up was the description of the truck and the boy Marcie had seen. "Would you like to tell me about this, Marcie?" he asked.

"Friday night that truck drove through one of our daylily fields. Aunt Jane called it in, and I've called since then, but no one has come out to investigate. As you can see, I got part of the license plate and a good description of the truck and one of the occupants."

She pointed to the paper the sheriff was holding. "I saw one of the passengers very clearly, and I can't imagine there is more than one truck with that paint job in this area. That orange dragon on the side was pretty distinctive."

"You saw an orange dragon on a white pickup?" Kyle Hughes asked sharply.

Marcie turned toward him and nodded. "Yes, I saw it clearly." She looked back to the sheriff. "The damage in parts of the field is severe, Ben. We can't be sure right now how many of the plants we can save, and Mr. Brookes, our insurance agent, said not to clean up or replant the plants that were uprooted but look viable until the damage was checked by this office. He thinks whoever is responsible can be forced to pay for at least part of the damage.

"The crops are insured, of course, but the insurance company would like to pursue the people responsible for the damage they caused. Fortunately they only drove through the one field. I'd like to start work in the field to see what I can save, but I'm waiting for someone from your office to come look at it first."

Ben Jamison turned a steely eye on the clerk and the deputy. "My policy is to check out every call that comes into this office. I hope I don't have to repeat myself on that score."

The sheriff was a soft-spoken man, but when he talked, those around him paid close attention. Marcie looked at the clerk to see how she had taken the sheriff's words, and she saw a flush cover the woman's cheeks. For some reason she didn't dare look at the deputy to see how he had taken the comment.

"I'm sorry, Marcie, that I wasn't here when your call came in. My wife and I were out of town. We cut our vacation short because my wife's arthritis is acting up. I'm still technically on vacation, but I came in today just to see what's going on. If I had been in the office when your call came in, we would have investigated immediately."

As the sheriff spoke, the clerk began gathering up the rest of the papers Marcie had dropped. She handed them to Marcie with an apologetic smile.

Sheriff Jamison smiled at the woman. "Thank you, Sarah. Would you please get me copies of the

logs of the calls Marcie Connor and Jane Southerland made to this office?" The sheriff's calm demeanor soothed the remnants of Marcie's anger.

The sheriff turned to the man standing silently
behind the desk. "You should look at this, Kyle."
He extended the page toward the deputy.

The deputy stepped around the desk and took the
paper from Sheriff Jamison. As he came to stand
beside the older man, Marcie was aware of just how
tall he was. At five feet, nine inches, Marcie was
not short, but this man was several inches taller. His
uniform shirt fit so well, she was sure it must have
been tailored just for him. She was keenly aware of
him, in a way she hadn't noticed any man in a long
time. He looked to be just a few years older than
she was, probably in his early thirties.

She noticed the width of his shoulders, the sub-
tle scent of his aftershave, and the fact that his blue
eyes no longer looked like ice chips. They were an
incredible blue, with small lines fanning out from
the corners that made her think he either spent a lot
of time in the sun or that he laughed often or both.
His dark brown hair was thick and shiny, with just
a hint of gray at the temples, and worn long enough
to brush his collar.

His body was solidly built, without any fat or
overly bulky muscles, and he moved gracefully
for such a big man. From the look of him, Marcie

decided he must spend a lot of time being active, not cooped up in his office behind a desk.

She clamped down on her awareness of him as a man, telling herself she had no room in her life for any man, no matter how attractive he was. Right now she needed a deputy, not a man, in her life.

His whole demeanor had changed, and he went very still as he read Marcie's description of the truck and passenger, almost as if he didn't even dare breathe.

Chapter Three

Quickly scanning the page, Kyle brought his attention back to Marcie. "You are quite sure of this description? You actually saw the truck and the boy yourself?" His voice had an edge to it, and Marcie couldn't stop a shiver that ran up her spine.

"Yes, I saw them. I had a good flashlight, and the moon was almost full. There was enough light to get a good look at the truck, and I saw the one boy very clearly."

"I'm sorry, Ms. Connor. I had no idea this was such a big deal." He had the grace to look contrite. "That didn't come out right. I should have investigated the incident, or sent someone out to investigate. Please forgive me."

He smiled, showing even white teeth against his

28

tan, and Marcie suddenly felt as if the sun had come out in the middle of a cloudy day. Once again she felt an unwelcome pull toward this man.

"I have a few calls to make. Please sit down. Would you like a cup of coffee?" he asked.

"Perhaps Marcie should come to my office, Kyle. I think you might want to make those phone calls in private." Sheriff Jamison gestured toward the door. "Come along with me, Marcie. I'll have Sarah bring the log entries to my office. Join us in my office as soon as you finish the calls, Kyle."

Marcie took one last look at the man seating himself behind his desk, feeling slightly bemused and off-kilter. She turned and followed the sheriff.

Sheriff Jamison met Sarah outside Deputy Hughes' office and took the log sheets from her. "Thanks, Sarah. Marcie and I will be in my office."

He escorted her along the hall to his office. "Would you like a soda or a cup of coffee? I'm going to start a pot of coffee. I probably drink too much of this stuff, but old habits are hard to break."

Marcie sat in one of the chairs in front of the sheriff's desk. "Actually, water would be good, Sheriff Jamison. I don't drink coffee, and I try to avoid soda."

He pulled a pitcher of water out of the dorm-sized refrigerator tucked under a counter along one wall. He poured some into a glass. After handing it to Marcie, he busied himself making a pot of coffee. Just as the sheriff sat in his chair, Deputy Sheriff Hughes came to the door.

"Ah, Kyle, come in. What did you find out?"

The deputy sheriff came into the room and took the seat next to Marcie.

As he lowered himself into the chair, Marcie noticed his expression and again felt a slight shivery feeling. She found herself almost compelled to stare at him, and she had the disturbing sensation that he felt her stare. She looked away quickly as he turned toward her, not wanting him to catch her at her close observation of him.

"Janie told me that the boys were out with the truck Friday until almost three in the morning. When she saw the truck Saturday morning, it was covered with mud. She asked them about it, and they told her they were out riding around but didn't tell her where they had been."

He took a deep breath. "I asked her to bring the boys by here as soon as they get out of school. She had some questions, but I just told her I wanted to talk to the boys." He let out the breath, and Marcie had a feeling he was having a hard time keeping his emotions in check.

"Can you stay here until school is out, Ms. Connor?" He turned his gaze on her, and Marcie felt the impact of that gaze all the way to her toes.

She looked at her watch. "I have a few errands to do, but I can come back. I'll call Aunt Jane and let her know I'll be a bit later than we planned. She'll be able to watch my children until I get home." She stood, as did both the men.

"Do you need to use the phone, Marcie?" Sheriff Jamison asked.

"Thank you, sheriff, but I've got my cell phone in the car." After saying good-bye, Marcie turned and walked to the door.

Both men stood where they were, with Kyle Hughes watching Marcie, and Sheriff Ben Jamison watching his deputy. The deputy missed Ben's speculative glance because he was too busy thinking about the beautiful woman who had just walked out the door.

Kyle wondered if she was married. She hadn't been wearing a wedding ring—he had checked her left hand. But she had mentioned children. Perhaps she didn't wear her ring. He thought about asking Ben but didn't want the older man to know he was interested.

Ben barely had time to wipe the beginnings of a smile off his face as Kyle turned toward him.

"I'm sorry, Ben, that I let you down. I had no idea people could make that much money selling plants. I thought it was just a few flowers in some old lady's garden. I should have investigated the incident, no matter the value of the plants involved."

The sheriff smiled and clapped him on the back. "No problem, Kyle. Just make sure you learn from your mistakes. Out here in the country, things are a little different from the cities you've worked in. Marcie Connor and Jane Southerland wouldn't have called us unless it was serious. Some folks might panic over little things, but, like I said, we need to investigate every call."

He walked across the room and sat down behind his desk. "We get our share of crank calls, just like any police department, and there are always calls I wish we could skip. But people depend on us to be there when they call and to take their complaints seriously." He picked up the papers Marcie had left on his desk.

"My wife has been buying plants from Harmony Farm for years. I can't tell you how much money we've spent there, or how much time I've spent planting the stuff she buys. At least she doesn't buy many plants with three-figure price tags."

Kyle sat down on the other side of the desk and glanced at the page the sheriff held up. It was a page of pictures of pink flowers, some with a deeper pink circle around the center and some with yellow or light green centers. The thought of paying over one hundred dollars for a plant stunned him. He wouldn't have been able to say what it was about the plants that made them special, and he really didn't see anything worth that kind of money.

If Ms. Connor hadn't said they were daylilies, he wouldn't have been able to identify them. What he knew about flowers came from calling a florist and ordering a bouquet. He remembered his mother and grandmother fussing about their flowers, but he hadn't really paid attention. The sheriff was right; things were very different here than anywhere he had worked before.

"She's a special kind of woman, Marcie Connor. Smart as well as beautiful. She and her brother have set up a Web site so they can sell their plants to customers all over the country. She was married, but unfortunately she married a man who couldn't control his drinking, his anger, or his fists. He left her with three kids to raise on her own. Walked out on her while she was carrying twins. The man was an idiot not to have seen what Marcie is worth."

Ben fixed his deputy with a sharp look that pinned Kyle in place.

"She might be open to dating again, if the right man came along."

Kyle wasn't sure if Ben was warning him away from Marcie or trying to tell him she was available. He thought about Ben's words for just a few seconds, then turned away from the shrewd older man.

"I think I'll go back to my office and try to get some paperwork done. I'll call you when Janie gets here with the boys."

Ben smiled as Kyle walked out of his office. He had seen the way he and Marcie Connor had looked at each other and had felt the sparks fly between them. His wife would tell him to mind his own business, but Ben didn't always do as his wife wanted. Perhaps a little matchmaking might be in order. Kyle was a good man, and Marcie a special woman. Maybe the two of them would make a good pair if given a chance.

Marcie finished her errands and drove back to the county facilities where the sheriff's office was located. She sat in her car, wondering whom Deputy Kyle Hughes had called. Who was Janie, and what was she to Kyle Hughes?

She had been trying to push those thoughts out of her head since walking out of the sheriff's office. And she really couldn't even have said why it was important to find out the answers. Hughes was someone she would probably never see once the investigation into the damage at the farm was completed. He was too arrogant, too forceful, and way too male to suit her. She decided that if Janie was his wife, the woman must like him just the way he was. Marcie clamped down hard on that thought, not sure why the image of Kyle Hughes with a wife bothered her.

Just because her own marriage hadn't worked out, she had no reason not to wish for happy marriages for others. Still, the thought of Kyle Hughes going home each evening to a wife who sat waiting for his return gave her a twinge somewhere in the region of her heart. Perhaps the boys he had spoken of were his sons. That would be a real kick in the pants, if it were true. How would a man like Kyle Hughes react if his own sons turned out to be the culprits?

Deciding she was wasting way too much time thinking about Kyle Hughes and whether or not he was married, Marcie took a deep breath and opened her car door. She walked up the sidewalk and the front steps to the county offices and went inside. She needed to focus on the fact that her property had been damaged and not let herself get distracted. Finding the culprits who had damaged the daylily field was the only issue that was important.

There was no one at the desk in the reception area, so Marcie waited for Sarah to come back. She wasn't aware that as she stood by the desk, a certain deputy sheriff was sitting behind his desk, hoping to catch a glimpse of her.

Chapter Four

Kyle Hughes sat at his desk, trying to concentrate on the paperwork in front of him. Unfortunately, the words on the pages didn't seem clear. The image of the woman he had spoken to earlier kept intruding into his thoughts.

He kept thinking she couldn't have been as pretty as he recalled. He remembered green eyes blazing with anger, and dark red hair. That much he knew was true. But could she have had the face of an angel, with a few freckles scattered over her nose? Or was he just remembering wrong? He gave a little snort of disgust. He should know better than to think of getting involved with a woman.

His own marriage had been cut short when his

wife died in a car crash caused by a drunk driver, and he'd waited a long time to date again. When he had finally started dating, he picked the wrong woman. He'd been thinking that they had something special going on between them and had even thought about proposing to her. Then he'd been called out to a local bar to break up a fight and found her in the center of it.

She had laughed at him when he'd arrested her for being drunk and disorderly. It hadn't been funny to him, and he'd sworn off women. For the last few years the only women in his life had been his mother, his grandmother, and his sister-in-law.

He thought about Ella, his late wife, fairly often, and found that the ache of loss was no longer as sharp as it once had been. But he missed having someone to come home to, someone who asked about his day and curled up with him on the couch to listen to the drops tapping on the roof on rainy days. He wondered what Marcie Connor did on rainy days, and if she liked marshmallows in her hot cocoa, and if she would make cookies for no other reason than to smell them baking.

It was funny. His brother had a wife and two kids he adored and a career in the Navy that kept him away from home for months on end. Kyle, with no one to keep him around, was the one with the settled job in a small town in middle America.

Why this encounter with this woman should be sticking in his mind was a puzzle. Oh, the circumstances under which he had met her were unusual, to be sure, and maybe that was why she seemed to be firmly implanted in his mind. How many women came to the law because their garden had been destroyed? At least, how many women under age sixty-five?

But then again, it could be the light floral perfume she had been wearing, or the fact that he liked competent, independent women. Or maybe the attraction was just because he hadn't been involved with a woman in over three years. Whatever it was, he vowed to put it out of his mind and concentrate on business.

Right, he thought. As if he could actually keep his mind on anything but Marcie Connor.

When Sarah returned to her desk, she sent Marcie back to Ben's office. As she walked past the door to the deputy sheriff's office, Marcie noticed that Kyle Hughes was sitting at his desk, staring at some papers laid out before him.

She stopped and watched him for a moment, taking in the lock of dark brown hair that fell over his forehead, the width of his shoulders, and the slightly crooked nose that kept his face from being too perfect. She decided it must have been broken once and wondered how it had happened.

He looked up and saw Marcie standing outside

his door. She flushed as he caught her staring and walked quickly away from the open doorway. Kyle felt a slight smile tug at his lips. She had been watching him. Maybe that was a good thing. He began whistling a tune as he stared at the papers on his desk. He wasn't seeing the words on the pages any better, but he didn't much care. Just knowing that Marcie Connor had been staring at him made his spirits rise. And, yes, she was as beautiful as he'd first thought.

Marcie and Sheriff Jamison were sitting in his office, talking about everything and the weather, when they heard Sarah Jones greet the woman and boys they were waiting to see.

"Hello, Mrs. Hughes. How are you today? Hello, James, Tom. Kyle is waiting for you in his office. Just go on back."

Mrs. Hughes. That answered Marcie's question. Janie *was* his wife. Oh, well, she wasn't looking for a man, anyway. She didn't need a man in her life. She had learned to stand on her own two feet, and she could take care of herself and her children without a man's help. Still, she couldn't help but feel a slight twinge of disappointment. She forced her attention back to the conversation, realizing that Sheriff Jamison was waiting for her to say something.

"I'm sorry, Sheriff. I was just thinking about the work I've got to do. I'm afraid I missed your last comment." She hoped he couldn't tell that she wasn't quite telling the truth.

The sheriff smiled. "That's quite all right, Marcie. We'll let Kyle talk to Janie Hughes for a few minutes before we go to his office. If you can identify the boy you saw on your property, we'll proceed from there."

Marcie thought about Kyle Hughes greeting his wife and decided she had either misread the fact that he seemed interested in her, or he was one of those men who needed to flirt with every woman he came into contact with. Like her ex-husband, who had never been able to confine his attention to her if there was another female within ten feet. She hoped Kyle Hughes didn't treat his wife so badly that she felt as worthless as Marcie herself had felt during her marriage. Knowing you were married to a man who just couldn't be faithful was a cancer that ate at a woman's soul.

A few minutes later they heard raised voices coming from the office next door. The heated discussion lasted several minutes; then a light knock sounded on the connecting door between the two offices. Kyle stuck his head in and asked them to please come into his office.

Marcie preceded the sheriff through the doorway and took in the woman sitting in the chair in front of the desk. She was obviously crying, and as soon as Marcie and the sheriff came into the room, she tried to pull herself together. Her sobs trailed off, and she blew her nose on a tissue gripped tightly in her hand.

As she looked up at them, Marcie realized that not even tears could detract from this woman's beauty. She was blonde, with large blue eyes made luminous by her tears. Her hair was styled in a French twist, with every hair in place. She projected an aura of fragility and seemed to be the type of woman who inspired men to want to protect her and do things for her. She was wearing an outfit that made Marcie feel positively dowdy by comparison. Her aqua suit looked like a designer outfit.

Perfectly manicured fingernails, painted pearl pink, made Marcie want to stick her own hands into the pockets of her skirt to hide her short fingernails, which she never grew long due to the hours she spent working in the gardens. She silently admonished herself to stand up straight and not worry about her fingernails. As long as she kept them clean, she shouldn't be ashamed that they were short. And if her hair had the tendency to resist her efforts to tame it, she wasn't going to feel ashamed for that, either.

The next person Marcie saw was a tall, thin young man standing by the door. He looked as if he might run out of the office at any moment. His resemblance to Kyle Hughes was easy to spot. He was definitely a younger, thinner version of the man standing uneasily behind the desk. As Marcie watched the young man, a gasp drew her attention to another boy standing by the window. As she turned toward the sound, she saw the boy who had been in the passenger seat of the pickup that had wrecked the daylily field.

She knew it was the boy she had seen in the truck, as his blue Mohawk haircut gave him away.

He seemed as surprised to see her as she was to see him. After his first gasp of surprise he clamped his lips shut and stared at the floor. He avoided looking at Marcie again, in contrast to the older boy, who glared at her from his place by the door. She stared back at him, slightly intimidated by his angry glare but not wanting to let him know how she felt.

Sheriff Jamison once again broke the tension. "Does either of these young men look familiar to you, Marcie?"

She nodded, barely able to draw a breath. For just a moment she couldn't seem to speak, and when she finally did, her words came out a little breathlessly. "Yes, Sheriff." She gestured toward the boy standing by the window. She took a deep breath and spoke more confidently. "He is definitely the boy I saw in the truck in the middle of the daylily field. He was the passenger closest to the door of the truck. You'll note I described him in my report as having a blue Mohawk haircut."

The silence after her pronouncement spun out for several seconds. Then the woman seated in front of the desk started crying again. Kyle stepped around the desk and placed his hands on her shoulders. She stood up, and he pulled her against him, putting his arms around her protectively.

"Please, Janie. Don't cry. Everything will be all right." He patted her back awkwardly, and Marcie was reminded of how she had tried to comfort her daughter just a few days earlier. It wasn't exactly the gesture of a man comforting his beloved wife, and Marcie wondered if there were problems between Kyle and Janie Hughes. If he was a constant flirt, it might explain the awkwardness.

She wasn't given long to think about that possibility, as the boy standing by the window started edging toward the door. Kyle spoke to him, and he stopped moving.

"Is there something you'd like to tell us, James?"

"I tried to tell him not to do it. It was Tom's idea." He looked quickly from the deputy to Marcie. "I'm sorry. I told Tom not to do it."

"Shut up, James! Just shut up!" the older boy yelled at his brother, taking a step toward him.

Kyle quickly stepped between the boys. "Why don't the two of you just settle down? Do you want to tell me what happened last Friday, Tom?" He laid a hand on the boy's arm, and Tom shrugged his hand away with an angry gesture.

Tom Hughes grabbed his brother by the front of his shirt. "I told you to keep your mouth shut, you jerk! They couldn't prove anything. You had to open your mouth, you little whiner."

"Tom, that's enough." Janie Hughes spoke quietly but loud enough for everyone to hear her. "Leave your brother alone. I want to know exactly what is going on, and I want to hear the truth. Do I hear it from your Uncle Kyle, or are you going to tell me?"

Marcie heard the words *Uncle Kyle* and almost missed what the boy had to say. Kyle and Janie weren't married. If Kyle was the boy's uncle, there was still a chance he wasn't married. She tried to clear her thoughts and concentrate on what was being said.

"Tom wanted to impress his girlfriend. I told him we should just go home, but he wouldn't listen to me." James looked as if he was on the verge of tears. Marcie almost felt sorry for the boy, but she thought about the damage the teens had caused and hardened her heart against the rush of tenderness she felt. Then she felt guilty for not having a more forgiving attitude and admonished herself to let go of the anger in her heart.

Janie Hughes spoke again. "I'm waiting for your explanation, Tom."

The boy stared defiantly at his mother for a few minutes, then began speaking.

"We were just out riding around. We went to Scooter's Place, where all the kids hang out, and had hamburgers and ice cream, and I saw Kate Bryant." He stopped at his mother's slight intake of breath.

"I know, I know. I'm not supposed to have anyone else in the truck with me except family. But Kate was with some other kids, and when she saw me, she asked for a ride. I wanted to show off for her, so I said yes. She lives out of town, on the way to that flower place. We were just riding around, and when we got to Kate's house, she said we should ride around some more. She didn't have to be home until midnight."

He took a deep breath. "I know—we were supposed to be home by eleven. I guess I really screwed up. Anyway, I kept driving past her house, and we turned off onto a dirt road. I didn't know where it went, and when we got to the sign that said Harmony Farm, I didn't know what it was. I thought the fields were empty. Kate didn't say anything about flowers, and James and I didn't know, but he did tell me not to drive in there. We went in and just drove around. When James saw the lady come out of the house, we took off. We left Kate at her house and went home."

Marcie couldn't believe her ears. This young man had destroyed thousands of dollars worth of plants so he could show off for a girl. And the worst part was that she knew the Bryant family. They had only lived in the area a few years, and Marcie didn't know them well. She did know who they were, though, and it hurt to know that someone local had been in the truck when it was driven through the daylily field.

"Thank you, Tom. I wish you had been honest with me on Saturday. You should have told me when I asked you about the mud all over the truck." Janie Hughes turned to Marcie. "I'm so sorry for the damage my sons caused."

Janie struggled to keep from crying. "What happens now? Will Tom be arrested?" She looked up at Kyle for reassurance.

He didn't answer her right away, and Marcie knew he must be carefully considering his words.

"There might be thousands of dollars worth of damage, Janie. I'm not sure what the outcome will be. I'll go out to Harmony Farm to investigate. If the owners decide to prosecute Tom, he may be held as an adult. That would be up to the judge."

Marcie wanted to look at Kyle, but she couldn't take her eyes off the two boys. The older boy seemed to be growing angrier by the minute, but his younger brother was staring at her with his mouth hanging slightly open.

Young James spoke again. "How can a few flowers be worth thousands of dollars?"

Kyle looked at Marcie and smiled slightly. He shook his head. "Please, let's not get into that again. I'll explain it to you later, James. For now, why don't we all take a ride out to your place, Ms. Connor?"

Kyle helped Janie to her feet, a steadying hand at her elbow. "You boys can ride with your mother and me in my car."

He pinned Tom with a look that Marcie was glad wasn't directed at her. "Don't even think of trying to get out of this, Tom. Ms. Connor and her family have suffered quite a bit of damage to their livelihood, and now it's time to see what can be done to make things right."

He turned and spoke to Marcie. "Lead the way, Ms. Connor. We'll follow you out to your place."

She nodded, and they proceeded outside to their cars. Marcie was too conscious of Deputy Sheriff Kyle Hughes following her as she drove to Harmony Farm. Luckily traffic was light, and it was an easy drive. Her nerves would have been really shot if she had had to drive much farther with the sheriff's department car following her.

It wasn't the fact that an officer of the law was

following her, as much as it was knowing who the particular officer was. She was still feeling that tug of instant attraction that seemed to flare up every time she looked into his eyes. And no matter how many times she told herself to ignore the feeling, she couldn't put it out of her mind.

Chapter Five

As they stopped at the damaged field, Marcie saw her parents' car parked beside the driveway. Her mother and father were walking in the field, surveying the ruins. As Marcie parked her car, her parents walked over to her. She got out and hugged her parents.

Kyle parked his car behind Marcie's and sat there a few moments talking to the boys before the four members of the Hughes family got out of the car. He was appalled by what he saw. The general neatness of the farm was marred only by the mess in the field Tom had driven through.

Marcie introduced her parents to the Hughes family but didn't have a chance to explain that Tom had been the driver of the truck. Kyle Hughes and

Andrew Greer shook hands, and Andrew gestured toward the field.

"I hope you'll be able to catch whoever did this, Deputy. I just can't imagine what they could have been thinking to do something like this." As he spoke, Janie Hughes started crying again, and Andrew looked at her in puzzlement.

Marcie stepped up to her father and laid a hand on his arm. "Uh, Dad, we need to talk." She led him away from the others a bit and quickly explained the situation.

Kyle and Janie stood by the garden, talking softly. Once again Kyle was trying to comfort her. Tom was standing by the car, but James had walked over to the edge of the field and was looking at the damage.

Andrew and Marcie walked slowly back to the others. Marcie stood beside her father as he addressed the small group.

"I'm sorry, folks. Marcie just explained what happened."

He walked to the cars, where Tom was standing. "Well, young man, what do you have to say for yourself?"

Tom stared at him defiantly, and Marcie found herself holding her breath. Her father wasn't a man to lose his temper, but Tom's attitude could possibly push even Andrew Greer to anger.

Tom stayed silent long enough for the moment

to become uncomfortable. Andrew shook his head and turned and walked away from the boy. James was still standing by the field, and Andrew walked over to him.

"Have you ever worked on a farm before, young man?"

"No, sir. I've never worked anywhere. I'm only fourteen."

Andrew Greer smiled. "Well, I'd say it's time for you to start working somewhere." He turned to Kyle and Janie Hughes. "I believe the best way to teach these young men the consequences of their actions will be to have them work for me. They can come out on weekends and days off from school for now. When school is out next summer, they can work full-time. If they agree to that and do a good job, without skipping out or slacking, I won't press charges."

Janie looked to Kyle for his reaction to Andrew Greer's offer.

"It sounds good to me, Janie." He turned to Tom, who still had not spoken. "Tom, you can drive out here every day that Mr. Greer specifies. If I hear that you aren't keeping your end of the bargain, I'll drive you out here myself."

Tom finally broke his silence. "You can't make me come out here. You're not my father!" He was shouting angrily. "You made the bargain, not me, and you can't force me to work on some stupid flower farm."

Kyle flinched at the boy's angry tirade. A muscle jumped along his jaw, and Marcie could see that he was trying not to show his anger at Tom's outburst. Before he could speak, Janie gently laid a hand on Kyle's arm.

"Tom, please don't." Her voice sounded weary. "We all know that Kyle isn't your father. He doesn't want to take your father's place. He's just trying to help us. Until your father is able to come home, you will listen to me and to your Uncle Kyle. You created this situation when you deliberately ruined someone else's property."

Janie took a deep breath and seemed to stand up just a little taller. "Now you are going to accept the consequences of your thoughtless actions. You will come here and work for Mr. Greer whenever he says, and if you don't, I will not try to stop him from pressing charges against you. Do you understand?"

The boy stared at his mother for a moment, then dropped his gaze toward the ground. His mumbled "yes" was almost inaudible.

"Be here next Saturday at nine. Wear clothes you won't mind getting dirty." Andrew Greer walked in front of James and stuck out his hand. James stared at it for a few heartbeats, then shook hands with the older man. As he turned to shake hands with Tom, Marcie's father winked at her.

Tom's expression was sullen, but he did shake hands with Andrew Greer.

She smiled as she watched her father dealing with the boys. He was such a naturally upbeat person, a real people person, that Marcie didn't doubt he would soon be great friends with both boys. If anyone could change Tom's surly attitude, it would be Andrew Greer.

After Kyle, Janie, and the boys left, Marcie and her mother and father stood by the field talking. Marcie scolded her parents for cutting their vacation short, knowing even as she did that nothing would have kept her father away from Harmony Farm any longer at this time. Andrew Greer was passionate about the plants they grew and sold, and his heart was always on the farm, no matter where he and Marcie's mother traveled. He often said he wasn't happy unless he had the dirt of Harmony Farm under his feet. Marcie knew exactly how he felt, as she felt the same way.

The three of them went to the house, where Marcie's children happily greeted their grandparents. After giving the children the small presents they had brought for them, Marcie's parents went on to their house. They planned to meet back at the garden as soon as they had all changed into work clothes in order to start trying to save the plants that could be salvaged.

The rest of the week passed in a flurry of activity as Marcie and the others labored on getting plants out of the damaged field. The whole field would have to be worked in order to smooth out the ruts left by the truck, but Andrew planned to have James and Tom Hughes help do that. For now it was enough to start removing plants and replanting them in another field Andrew had prepared for the daylily seedlings that were now growing in the greenhouses.

The hybridizing of plants was an exciting process to Marcie and her parents. They chose the parent plants carefully, with an idea of what the cross might produce, but the results were often quite different from what they imagined. They had created many beautiful new color combinations over the years, and Marcie was often amazed that they could continue to find names for the new plants. They would have to prepare another field for the seedlings still in the greenhouses. Luckily the weather in this part of central Arkansas allowed for the planting of daylilies until late in the fall.

On Saturday morning a few minutes before nine, Tom Hughes drove up the driveway and parked alongside the field. Marcie, Andrew, and Sharon were waiting for the boys to arrive. Andrew had an assortment of shovels and rakes laid out at the edge of the field, and a tractor sitting on the drive.

As the boys got out of the truck, Andrew greeted them. "Good morning, boys." He went on to tell them what they would be doing and what he expected of them. He made no mention of the fact that they were at the farm under inauspicious circumstances, nor did he act as if he held a grudge against them. He treated them as he would any new employee, taking time to carefully explain the tasks at hand, letting them ask questions, and treating them courteously.

The five of them worked steadily, with Andrew directing. As he watched the boys working, he made sure they didn't get too tired their first day, having them take short, frequent breaks to rest and catch their breath. There was a cooler with soft drinks and bottled water available, and Andrew made sure the boys stayed hydrated. Sharon had baked cookies the night before and brought some of them with her.

James was full of questions, and Andrew, Sharon, and Marcie found themselves telling the story of Harmony Farm and explaining about the plants they grew. James was amazed at the idea of making a living through selling plants, and as Andrew explained things to him, James caught on easily and worked with both interest and great enthusiasm.

Tom wasn't as interested in either the story of Harmony Farm or the work, but as the morning wore on, he did as he was asked without complaint. He rarely spoke to the others and didn't ask questions except for those pertaining to the work he was doing.

When they took their lunch break, Marcie walked to her house, and her parents took James and Tom to their house. As the others walked away, Marcie could still hear James asking questions and her father cheerfully answering them. The two of them were becoming great friends, and Marcie was impressed by the way the boy soaked up everything her father told him. James was articulate and quick-witted, quite likeable in spite of his blue Mohawk.

After lunch Marcie showered and changed and left to go into town to do some shopping. She took Emily with her but left the twins at home with Aunt Jane, who was baking cookies. All three of the children enjoyed helping Jane in the kitchen, but Emily needed some art supplies and wanted to accompany her mother on the shopping trip.

Emily stared at the boys working in the field next to her grandparents as they drove past. Marcie watched her in the rearview mirror and was sad to note the expression on Emily's face. Emily wasn't happy to see those boys with her grandparents.

Chapter Six

As she drove along the dirt lane leading from Harmony Farm to the main road, Marcie saw a sheriff's department car coming toward her. She slowed as she passed it, and when the car stopped just beyond hers, she pulled over to the shoulder. As the car made a U-turn and pulled up behind her, she realized that the driver was Kyle Hughes.

He got out of his car and walked up beside Marcie's. His smile did funny things to Marcie's insides, and she wasn't quite sure what to make of the electricity that seemed to emanate from him. She tamped the fluttery feeling down and smiled at him.

"Good morning, Deputy. What brings you out this way?"

As he looked down at Marcie, Kyle Hughes was

struck again by her beauty. Her glorious auburn hair was pulled up onto her head in a style reminiscent of a long-ago age, with a few loose tendrils falling down here and there. He remembered seeing his grandmother with her hair fixed like Marcie's, but on Marcie the style looked anything but grandmotherly. Kyle wondered if it would feel as silky as it looked, and he barely resisted the urge to reach out and touch it.

The expression on Marcie's face changed from a warm smile to one of puzzlement, and Kyle realized he was staring at her without a clue as to what to say to her. He pulled his wayward thoughts away from her hair and tried to form a coherent sentence.

"I was just on my way out to your place to make sure the boys had arrived on time. I wouldn't have come, but Janie asked me to make sure everything was okay."

"They arrived on time this morning, and when I left, everything was fine. James and Dad are getting on as if they've known each other forever." She didn't mention Tom, and Kyle picked up on the omission.

"What about Tom? I hope he isn't causing trouble." His voice reflected the doubt he felt about Tom's ability to do what was asked of him.

"Tom is quiet, but he is working. I think if anyone can get the best out of him, it will be my dad. We've had quite a few high school and college kids work for us over the years, and my dad is very patient and easy to get along with. He won't let Tom skate through this, but he won't be overly hard on him, either."

Emily stirred restlessly in the backseat, and Marcie turned to her.

"We'll go in just a minute, sweetheart." She looked back at Kyle. "Maybe you shouldn't go out to the farm, Deputy. Let my father and the boys work this out between them." She smiled to take any sting out of her words, not wanting him to think she was criticizing him.

"You may be right, Ms. Connor. Now that I've talked to you, I don't need to go out there to see for myself. I can reassure Janie that the boys are keeping their part of the bargain." He touched two fingers to his hat in a small salute and stepped away from the car. "I hope to see you again, Ms. Connor."

As he turned to walk back to his car, Marcie stopped him by saying, "Deputy Hughes?" She smiled as he turned toward her. "You're welcome to call me Marcie."

His smile hit her like the sun coming out from behind the clouds after a rain shower.

"I will, if you'll call me Kyle." As he walked to his car, he was whistling, a fact that was not lost on Marcie or her daughter.

"Who is that man, Mom?" Emily was turned around as far as her seat belt would allow, trying to

get a look at the tall man her mom had been talking to.

Marcie explained to Emily that Deputy Sheriff
Kyle Hughes was the man from the sheriff's office
who had come out to investigate the damage to the
daylilies. She told Emily that he was also the uncle
of the boys who had done the damage.

"I don't like him, then. I don't like those boys,
either." Emily spoke decisively.

Marcie chose her words carefully before she
replied. "But you don't know them, sweetheart. The
boys are working with your grandmother and grandfather to fix the damage they did. The deputy sheriff can't help it if the boys did a bad thing. It isn't
his fault. We have to give them a chance to make
up for what they did. They did a bad thing, but they
aren't bad people. Maybe when we get back from
town, you can go out to the field where they're
working and meet them."

Emily shook her head. "No, thanks, Mom. I
don't want to meet them."

Marcie didn't know what to say in the face of
Emily's adamant refusal. She changed the subject
by talking about their shopping trip and let the subject of the Hughes family drop. They spent the next
two hours getting the things on their shopping list,
then headed home.

When Marcie and Emily returned to the farm, the
field was empty of people and machinery. Marcie

drove up to her house, parking around back. As they carried their purchases into the house, they heard laughter coming from her parents' patio. The houses were close together, separated only by gardens and lawn, and Marcie realized it must be James she heard laughing. They could also hear a dog barking, and Marcie realized it was Emily's black and white border collie, Patches.

They set their shopping bags on the porch steps, and Emily ran across the lawn to her grandparents' house. As she came up onto the patio, Emily saw James Hughes tossing a ball for Patches. The dog ran and grabbed the ball, bringing it back to James.

"Patches, come here, girl." Emily ran to the dog, and Patches dropped the ball at the little girl's feet. Emily took the dog by the collar and started pulling her toward home. "Come on, girl. Let's go home." She cast a hateful look at James and walked away with the dog following her.

"Emily, wait just a minute." Marcie stood in front of her daughter, blocking her way. "Emily, that wasn't nice. James was playing with Patches. You should have let him continue. I think you owe him an apology."

Emily looked up at her mother with eyes shiny with unshed tears. "But I don't want him to play with Patches! I hate him! I want him to just go to jail!" She folded her arms across her chest and glared at her mother stubbornly.

Marcie dropped to her knees in front of her daughter. She pulled the girl into her arms. "Oh, sweetheart, please don't be so angry. I told you, James and Tom may have done a bad thing, but they aren't bad people. I want you to be nice to them."

Emily pulled away from her mother with a sob and ran toward the house. Marcie watched her go, not knowing if she should make her come back or let her go. Patches ran after the girl, following her to the house.

Sharon stepped up beside her daughter and laid a hand on her arm. "Let her go, Marcie. She's angry and confused. Things will sort themselves out."

Marcie smiled at her mom. "I hope so, Mom. She's had a lot to deal with, and I don't like to see her upset. But I can't let her be rude, either."

Sharon slipped one arm around Marcie's waist and hugged her. "It will all work out. You'll see."

Marcie hugged her mother back. She stepped away and said, "I've got to get to the house and put away my groceries. See you later." She smiled and waved at her father, who sat on the patio with the Hughes boys.

That evening Marcie answered her phone, not recognizing the number that showed on her caller ID. She immediately recognized the voice of the caller, though.

"Hi, Marcie. Kyle Hughes. I just wanted to let you know that Janie just called me. She said the boys can't stop talking about your parents. Both of them were pretty impressed with your dad. He offered to take them over to your brother's to see his horses. He told them there might be a chance of their getting to work with your brother. Tom is excited about the horses, and James is over the moon about working with your dad. He seems to have adopted your dad as a surrogate grandfather."

Marcie wasn't quite sure what to say. His next words left her even more at a loss for words.

"I really am sorry, Marcie, that I didn't take your complaint more seriously. I should have investigated your calls right away. I hope you won't hold it against me, as I'd like to see you again."

"I'm sure we will be seeing each other, since your nephews will be working for my dad." As Marcie thought about seeing Kyle again, her heart seemed to pick up speed.

There was a brief silence at the other end of the line, and then Kyle continued. "Actually, I was thinking more of seeing you alone sometime. I'd like to take you out to dinner or a movie."

He sounded a little hesitant, and Marcie wondered if he had a soft spot under his gruff exterior.

"I realize we didn't exactly get off to a good start, but I'd like to make it up to you. And I do want to see you again, just the two of us," he continued.

While she was flattered to think he might be interested in her, Marcie didn't answer right away. She had to think about more than just herself, and she didn't know if she was ready to actually go on a date just yet. Oh, she had often thought about how nice it would be to have someone special in her life, but she wondered if it would be right for her to start seeing Kyle Hughes. He was, after all, the uncle of the boys who had caused so much destruction to the plants she and her family depended on for their livelihood. She had noticed how Emily had reacted to seeing James playing with the dog. What would Emily think if she saw her mother start dating the boys' uncle?

"I guess your silence says it all. I'm sorry to have bothered you. I'll say good night now."

"Kyle, wait a minute. I'm sorry. I was just thinking of my children. Especially Emily, as she isn't too happy about the boys being here. This can't be just about you and me. I have children to think of." She paused to consider what she wanted to say. "I haven't dated since my divorce. I have to think about how everything I do affects my children. I'd like to see you again, and not just in the context of our involvement because of what the boys did, but we are going to have to take this really slowly."

She laughed a bit self-consciously. "You're probably thinking I'm taking your call way too seriously. You asked me about a possible dinner date or movie, not a lifetime commitment." She took a deep breath. "I'd like to have dinner with you some evening. Did you have a particular night in mind?"

"I'm off work Tuesday, if that would work for you. And believe me, I do understand what you're going through."

He paused, and when he spoke again, Marcie detected a note of sadness that wasn't in his voice earlier.

"I'll pick you up at about seven on Tuesday. Good night, Marcie."

As she hung up the phone, Marcie wondered about Kyle Hughes. She really didn't know much about him, she thought. Maybe she was making a mistake to get involved with him. But now was not the time to start second-guessing herself. She felt something when she was with him that she hadn't felt in a long time.

Considering how her marriage had turned out, Marcie didn't really trust herself when it came to dealing with men. Jim Connor had swept her off her feet, and look how that had turned out. His surface charm had worn thin quickly, then disappeared so completely that Marcie wondered if she had simply missed the clues that should have warned her away from him.

On the other hand, this was just a dinner date, not a major commitment. She could go to dinner with Kyle Hughes and see what happened from there. If she didn't enjoy herself, she wouldn't have to see him again.

Chapter Seven

Tuesday evening when Kyle knocked on the door, Jane Southerland answered. Marcie's twins, Seth and Laurel, ran into the foyer to see who was at the door. They stopped short at the sight of the large man who stepped into the house.

Jane informed Kyle that Marcie would be down momentarily and invited him into the living room. Just as she showed him into the large, comfortably furnished room, the phone rang, and she excused herself to go answer it.

He sat down on the couch, feeling somewhat disconcerted as the twins immediately climbed up beside him.

"I'm Seth. I'm five." The boy held up five fingers. He pointed to his twin sister. "Laurel's five too. She won't talk to you. She doesn't talk to strangers. I like trucks. Do you drive a truck?"

The little girl smiled shyly at Kyle. He noticed she favored her mother, with green eyes and reddish-blonde hair. Before he could reply, Marcie walked into the room.

Kyle stood up quickly. He took one look at Marcie, and his eyes widened in appreciation. She was wearing a blue and green print dress in a silky fabric. The full skirt swished around her long legs as she walked, and the colors of the dress looked fantastic on her. He had to remind himself to breathe as she walked closer to him.

"Hi. I'm sorry I wasn't down here to greet you. I hope the twins haven't talked your ear off." She smiled as she said it and ruffled Seth's hair as he jumped off the couch and hugged her around the legs.

Kyle was once again aware of the electric feeling that seemed to come over him every time he was near Marcie.

He smiled that smile that turned Marcie's insides to mush.

"Uh, no, the kids are great." He felt as tongue-tied as a teenaged boy asking a girl for their first date.

They stared at each other, the silence stretching out, lost in the wonder of the moment, until Marcie became aware that Seth was tugging on her skirt.

She looked down at her son, barely able to drag her eyes away from Kyle.

"Mommy, you look pretty. Can Laurel and I go with you?"

Marcie shook her head, clearing away the spell Kyle seemed to have cast upon her. "Not tonight, Seth. You and Laurel and Emily and Aunt Jane are going to watch a movie and make popcorn."

Seth looked up at her with disappointment on his face. Before he could say anything else, Jane came into the room.

Jane looked from Marcie to Kyle. "Well, you two need to get going." She reached for Seth's hand, then held out her other hand toward Laurel. "Come on, you two. It's time for our movie and popcorn. And once the movie is over, it will be time for your baths and a bedtime story."

The twins both said good-bye to Marcie and Kyle and went with Jane. As they left the room, chattering about the movie they were to watch, Marcie smiled at Kyle. "Shall we go?"

"I don't want you to go, Mommy! I want him to go away!"

Marcie spun around and stepped away from Kyle as she realized that Emily was in the doorway. The look on her daughter's face told Marcie that Emily was not happy about seeing her and Kyle together.

"Emily, we talked about this. I have a date with Kyle, and we are going out to dinner."

"I don't want you to go to dinner with him. I don't like him." Emily's lower lip jutted out as she began to pout. Her expression told Marcie that her daughter hadn't really accepted the fact that Marcie was going to dinner with Kyle.

"You don't know Kyle yet, Emily. We've talked about this. I will talk to you tomorrow. Now, please go watch the movie with your brother and sister." Marcie spoke quietly but with a firm tone to her voice.

Emily stared at Kyle and her mother for a moment, then turned and ran up the stairs. Marcie took a few deep, calming breaths. She felt Kyle's hand on her arm. Turning to him, she saw the concern in his eyes.

"Maybe we shouldn't do this, Marcie. If you want to call it off, I'll understand." His hand slipped off her arm, and he stepped back, leaving her feeling slightly chilly after the warmth of his touch and the nearness of his body.

"I explained to Emily that I was going to go to dinner with you. I don't think she would have objected to my going out with anyone else. It's just because of who you are. She has to accept the fact that I can have a life outside of being her mother and that even though James and Tom did something bad, it isn't your fault." She walked out of the room, and he followed her. As she took a light coat from the hall closet, he reached for it. She handed it to him, and he held it for her.

She slipped her arms into the coat, and Kyle smoothed it over her shoulders. He gently lifted her hair outside the collar of the coat, then let his hands rest lightly on her shoulders.

Marcie felt a strong urge to just lean back against Kyle. She wanted to let someone else be strong and support her. She wanted things she hadn't thought about in a long time. Someone to laugh with, to share a cup of hot chocolate with on a cool fall evening, someone to curl up with on the couch who could hold her and who didn't smell like children's bubble bath.

She ruthlessly squelched her thoughts, stepped away from him, and walked out the door. Taking a deep breath of the cool air that hit her as she stepped out onto the porch, Marcie hoped the air was cooling her cheeks as well as her lungs. She felt flushed all over and hoped it wouldn't show when she looked at Kyle again.

Kyle followed her, and they walked to his car in silence. He opened and held the passenger side door for her, and Marcie got into the car. She didn't fasten her seat belt at first. It was only as Kyle fastened his own that Marcie was able to put her thoughts away and fasten her own belt. She almost asked him to give her a rain check on the dinner but decided to go ahead with it. She and Emily would have to have a talk about what had happened, but for now she was going to try to enjoy her evening out.

Marcie and Kyle were sitting in Kent's Steak House, waiting for their dinner, when Marcie's cell phone rang. She had set her purse at her feet, and she reached for her phone, frowning as she saw the number displayed. "Hello, Aunt Jane. Is something wrong?"

"Marcie, I'm so sorry to disturb you. I can't find Emily. She watched the movie with us, and after I gave the twins their bath, she was in your bedroom, sitting on your bed. I asked her if she wanted to come and listen to the bedtime story I was going to read to the twins, but she said no. She said she was going to lie down in your room. I didn't think you would mind, so I said it was okay. When I finished reading to the twins, she was gone. I checked her room, and she wasn't there, either. I've looked all over the house, and I can't find her."

"I'll be there as soon as I can, Aunt Jane. Are the twins asleep?" Marcie paused as her great-aunt answered her question. "Okay, you stay there with them. Call Mom and Dad and Jack and Nancy. Emily may have snuck out and gone to one of their houses."

She hung up and replaced the phone in her purse.

"I have to go, Kyle. Emily is missing." She stood and picked up her purse.

Kyle also stood and helped her into her coat, which he had draped over one of the extra chairs at their table. He threw some bills onto the table just as their waitress returned.

"I'm sorry. Something has come up, and we need to leave." He indicated the money on the table. "I'm sure that will be enough to cover the bill, and you can keep the change."

They left the restaurant quickly, and Kyle drove back to Marcie's as fast as he dared.

At one point he smiled and squeezed her hand. "At least if I get pulled over for speeding, I can honestly say it's a police emergency."

Marcie smiled back at him, but he could tell she was worried about her daughter.

"She'll be all right, Marcie. We'll find her." He reached over and took her hand, giving it a reassuring squeeze. She didn't pull her hand away, and he held on as he drove.

When they pulled up in front of Marcie's house, her parents' car and her brother's truck were parked in front. Kyle parked his Jeep Grand Cherokee behind the truck, and Marcie was out of it and running for the house almost before the vehicle stopped. Her mother met her on the porch.

"Have you found Emily yet?" Marcie sagged as her mother shook her head, and Kyle came up behind her and put his arms around her, steadying her and keeping her from falling. He helped her into the house and led her into the family room, where just a short time earlier he and the twins had sat on the couch waiting for her.

"I've got to go look for her." Marcie tried to pull away from Kyle, but he pushed her gently onto the couch.

"Stay here, Marcie, in case she comes back. I'll go speak to your father, find out where they've looked so far." She struggled against him, and he dropped down next to her. "Is there any place she would hide? A favorite place the others might not know about?"

Kyle took her hands in his, and as Marcie gripped his fingers, her nails bit into his palms. She was white-faced, all her natural color drained away by the strain of not knowing where her daughter was.

"Think, Marcie. Where would she go?" Kyle brushed the hair away from Marcie's face, and she looked at him with such an anguished expression in her eyes that he felt his heart drop into his boots.

She shook her head. "I don't know, Kyle. She's never done anything like this before. I shouldn't have gone out. I knew she was upset. I should have stayed home with her." She looked down at her hands, which were still clenched in his.

He touched her cheek gently, lifting her face up. "We'll find her, Marcie." He bent and brushed a light kiss against her temple, then stood and left the room without a backward glance.

Sharon Greer sat down next to her daughter. Slipping her arms around Marcie, she tried to soothe her. Jane came into the room, carrying a tray with cups and a pot of the herbal tea she and Marcie both liked. She set the tray on the table in front of the couch and sat next to Marcie.

"I'm so sorry, Marcie. I've failed you." Jane was crying, and the sound of her anguish broke through to Marcie.

She turned to Jane and hugged her. "No, Aunt Jane. You're not to blame for this. I knew Emily was upset, and I shouldn't have left."

Sharon poured tea into three cups and set the cups on the table, but none of the women reached for one.

Jane Southerland spoke softly. "You can't blame yourself, Marcie. You have to have a life, some time just for yourself. You need to get out sometimes without the children. I should have watched her. I didn't realize she was so upset. After my daughter called, I was thinking about my own problems, and once I went upstairs with the twins, I didn't pay enough attention to Emily."

"What is it, Aunt Jane? Has something happened to Linda or one of her children?" Sharon asked.

"No, everyone is fine. But Linda has called me several times lately, telling me that I shouldn't stay here. She thinks I should move closer to her and her family. But I know she's just mad at me for moving here in the first place. She's feeling guilty because she and her children didn't have much time for me for the last few years before I came here to live. She's trying to assuage her feelings by telling me I work too hard here and hinting that I'm being taken advantage of."

Marcie looked at her great-aunt closely. "I'm so sorry, Aunt Jane. Are we asking too much of you? I know how much you do for us, and I depend on you to be here for the kids. Maybe we are taking advantage of you."

"Nonsense, Marcie. I love living here with you and the children. I feel needed and wanted and loved here. If Linda had had her way, she would have just put me away somewhere after I broke my arm. You and the children have given me a new lease on life." Jane gripped Marcie's hand tightly. "I don't want to change my life one bit. I told Linda that, and I've told her that every time she calls. I just wish I had paid more attention to Emily tonight. I feel like I've failed you."

Marcie hugged the older woman. "You didn't fail us, Aunt Jane. You aren't to blame." Before she had a chance to say anything else, the front door opened, and Marcie's brother, Jack, burst into the room.

"Marcie, we found Emily!"

He was followed by their father, who carried

Emily in his arms. Kyle came next, then Nancy, with Patches following closely behind. As Marcie's father placed Emily into her mother's arms, the dog jumped up onto the couch beside them.

"Get down, Patches." Marcie gently pushed the wet, muddy dog off the couch.

"Thank you, Dad. Where did you find her? How did you find her?" She took Emily into her arms without even giving a thought to the dress she was wearing, which was now getting dirty from the girl's clothing.

Emily looked fearfully from her mother to Kyle, who was standing just behind her grandfather. Burying her face against her mother's neck, Emily began crying softly.

"We heard the dog barking and followed the sound. Patches was outside one of the greenhouses, running back and forth in front of the door, barking. Kyle was the one who realized the dog wanted to go inside, and as soon as he opened the door, she ran in and went straight to Emily." He bent and scratched Patches behind one ear.

Andrew Greer smiled. "Emily was hiding under a workbench in the greenhouse. She and Patches are muddy because she found the one spot in the old greenhouse that gets wet every time it rains for more than a few hours at a time."

He helped Marcie to stand. "You need to get her upstairs and into dry, warm clothes. I'll take Patches and towel her off and give her a couple of dog treats." He hugged his daughter and kissed his granddaughter on the cheek. "Come on, Patches, let's go get you cleaned up." As he turned to go out of the room, Andrew asked, "Who wants coffee?"

Jack and Nancy both shook their heads. "Thanks, but we need to get home. We'll see you all tomorrow." They both hugged Sharon and Marcie and left.

The three women went upstairs, leaving Kyle and Andrew in the living room.

"Come with me, Kyle," Andrew said. "I know Marcie will want to talk to you as soon as she gets Emily settled."

"Perhaps I should leave, sir. It seems that what happened tonight was my fault. If I hadn't come to take Marcie out to dinner, Emily wouldn't have run away."

"Maybe so, young man, but I know Marcie doesn't hold you responsible, and you shouldn't blame yourself, either." The older man rubbed down the dog with some paper towels, then busied himself making a pot of coffee. "My daughter hasn't shown any interest in dating since her divorce. It's high time she started. Her mother and I were glad to hear she had a date tonight." He smiled at Kyle. "Oh, we know enough to stay out of Marcie's business. She would have a fit if she knew I was talking to you like this."

Andrew Greer set two cups on the counter and filled them with the fresh-brewed coffee. "Are you hungry? I bet you and Marcie didn't even get to eat your dinner."

Just then Sharon Greer came into the kitchen and heard her husband's question. Kyle tried to politely refuse the offer of food, but Sharon waved away his objections and went to the refrigerator to see what was available. She busied herself making roast beef sandwiches from the remains of a pot roast Marcie had cooked for supper the day before.

When Marcie walked into the kitchen a short time later, she found her parents and Kyle sitting around her kitchen table. They were talking as easily as if they had always known one another, and Marcie was proud of her parents for making Kyle feel at home. Kyle looked a bit uneasy to be sitting in the kitchen eating, and he started to apologize.

Marcie smiled, setting him at ease. "Since our dinner date was ruined, the least we can do is feed you." She sat down next to him. "Emily is sleeping. I think she'll be okay. She wasn't out in the cold very long, thanks to you two." She indicated her father and Kyle. "Thank you."

Sharon set another plate in front of Marcie, who stared at the sandwich for a few minutes before realizing she was hungry. "Thanks, Mom."

As Kyle and Marcie ate their sandwiches, her parents said good night and left. Marcie started to get up to walk them to the door, but both her mother and father bade her stay with Kyle and eat. She saw the looks her parents exchanged and wondered what they were thinking.

"They didn't give you the third degree did they?" she asked as she sat back down.

He didn't answer her immediately, and Marcie realized her words had made him a bit uncomfortable. She reached out and touched his arm lightly. "I'm sorry, Kyle. My dad said something about us, didn't he?"

Kyle thought about what he was going to say and smiled. "Your dad seems to think it's high time you started dating. I'd like to ask you out again, if tonight hasn't soured you on the idea of seeing me."

She nodded shyly, and they chatted idly while they finished eating their sandwiches. After clearing the table, Marcie asked Kyle if he would like more coffee. He declined, stating he had to leave as he had to be at work early the next morning. Marcie walked with him to the door.

They stood just inside the doorway, and as Marcie said good night, Kyle put his hands gently on her shoulders. "As first dates go, this wasn't exactly what I had in mind. Maybe our next date should include your children."

She smiled wryly. "I'm sure we can think of something. Good night, Kyle."

"Good night, Marcie. I'll call you." He walked out the door and shut it softly behind him.

Marcie locked the door, turned off all the lights, and went upstairs. Standing next to her daughter's bed, Marcie gently smoothed the hair back from Emily's face. Emily stirred but didn't wake up, and Marcie went to her room and got ready for bed. Did she want to see Kyle Hughes again? Even if they did something with the children, she wasn't sure it would be the right thing to do.

Chapter Eight

For so many years now she had been a single mother, denying that she might have need of the love and companionship of a man in her life. She had been giving all her time and attention to her children. She hadn't allowed herself to think about having or wanting a man in her life. Now, just when she seemed to have convinced herself that she was doing all right without male companionship, Kyle Hughes had come along.

And, wanting more than what she had now, could she find a way to bring Kyle into her life, and her children's lives, knowing how Emily felt? Would it be fair to them, and to him, if things didn't work out? Maybe she was making too much of the fact that he'd said he would like to see her again. She finally drifted off to sleep without answers to any of her questions.

Morning came way too soon to suit her, and the face that stared back at her from her mirror reflected her lack of sleep. Dark circles didn't do a thing to enhance her looks. Oh, well. There was no reason to worry about her looks. She wasn't planning to see Kyle today and didn't expect to encounter anyone outside her family.

The twins rushed into the kitchen, full of energy as always. They were ready to go to their preschool. As Marcie flipped pancakes for them, she marveled at their energy. Once they were settled with their breakfast, Marcie went upstairs to see if Emily was up. She hoped her eldest would be ready to go to school. Usually Emily enjoyed school, and she really liked her teacher, so perhaps today would be a normal day. Marcie hoped so.

Emily was up but not dressed. She was sitting on her bed, idly playing with a scruffy teddy bear that had been a long-ago birthday present.

"Hi, sweetheart. You need to get dressed now. The bus will be here in half an hour." Marcie sat on the bed next to Emily.

"Are you mad at me, Mom?" Emily hadn't looked at Marcie yet, keeping her eyes on the bear in her lap. "Are you going to punish me?"

"No, Emily, I'm not mad at you. I'm a little disappointed that you ran off and hid. Everyone was worried about you, and you could have been hurt. I want you to promise me that you won't ever do that again. I want you to remember that you can always talk to me about anything that's bothering you. Maybe you won't always like what I say, but we can always talk about anything." Marcie took a deep breath. "What sort of punishment do you think would be fitting for your actions?"

Emily didn't answer right away, and Marcie reached out to tip her chin up. One look at her daughter's face told Marcie there would be no punishment.

Gathering her daughter close, Marcie hugged her and said, "For one thing, you need to promise never to run away again, and you need to apologize to everyone who was worried about you. Punishment is the last thing on my mind right now. I'm just glad you weren't hurt. If you feel like running away again, I want you to remember how everyone felt last night when we didn't know where you were."

Emily dropped the bear and hugged her mother. "I'm sorry, Mom. I didn't want everyone to worry about me. I'll tell Grandma and Grandpa and Aunt Jane and Uncle Jack and Aunt Nancy that I'm sorry."

"There's one more person you need to apologize to. Kyle Hughes. He had to pay for a very nice dinner that we didn't get to eat. I know you didn't want me to go out with him, but he was also worried about you. And he brought me home as soon as Aunt Jane called us, and he went out with your grandfather to look for you."

She stood up and started getting clothes out of Emily's closet. "Now let's get you dressed so you don't miss the school bus."

Later that evening, after dinner, Marcie and Emily were washing dishes when the phone rang. Emily answered it, and Marcie noticed she didn't look happy when she heard the caller's voice. When Marcie heard Emily say, "Before I get my mom, I have something to say to you," she knew it was someone who had been at the house the previous evening. Since Emily had already apologized to everyone but Kyle, Marcie knew it had to be he.

As she listened to Emily apologize for ruining last night's dinner, Marcie felt her heart swell with pride. Her daughter had done exactly as Marcie had asked. She had apologized to everyone concerned, and done it sincerely. Emily handed her the phone, and Marcie dropped a gentle kiss on the top of her head and watched her daughter go back to the sink to finish washing the dishes.

"Hello, Kyle. How are you?"

Kyle heard the happiness in Marcie's voice and pictured her with her children. He knew how important her kids were to her, and not for the first time he regretted the way his own marriage had ended. He had always thought he and his wife would have three or four kids, and he felt infinite sadness that she had died before they could have even one.

"I'm fine, Marcie. I just wanted to touch base with you and make sure Emily was okay after last night. I also wanted to ask if you might want to take the kids out for pizza on Saturday."

"Emily is fine, thank you. And I'm sure the kids would love to go out for pizza."

"I'm glad you haven't changed your mind about seeing me again."

Marcie heard the uncertainty in his voice and replied, "I'd better warn you, I plan to eat my share of pizza. And I'm not sure how long it's been since you've taken three small children out to dinner, but you might be surprised at how much two five-year-olds can eat. I hope you won't regret asking by the end of the evening."

He laughed, and Marcie felt a thrill go through her at the sound. "I love pizza, I like kids, and I'm looking forward to Saturday. I'll pick you up at about six."

"Are you sure you don't want us to meet you in town? That way you won't have to drive all the way back out here after we eat."

"No, ma'am. My mother would have a fit if I didn't pick you up and deliver you back to your door at the end of the evening." He was definitely laughing now.

"How about if you meet us at my house and we take my car? I need booster seats for the kids. I'll let you drive, though, if that will make you feel better."

"You're right, Marcie. We probably should take your car. I'll see you Saturday. Good night."

As she hung up the phone, Marcie was smiling. She looked across the kitchen to see Emily watching her, and her smile slipped a bit.

"Thanks for helping me with the dishes, Emily. Let's sit and talk for a minute." She pulled a chair out from the table and gestured for Emily to sit down.

"I know you aren't happy about my going out with Kyle Hughes. Is it because he's Tom and James' uncle, or is it because you don't want me to go out with anyone?"

Emily didn't answer and wouldn't even meet her mother's eyes. She stared down at her hands, which were clenched together tightly in her lap.

Marcie saw a tear drop from her daughter's eye. She quickly knelt next to Emily's chair. "Don't cry, sweetheart." She put her arms around the child and laid her cheek on top of Emily's head. "Please tell me what's bothering you, Emily. I can't help if I don't know what's wrong."

"Those boys drove through the fields, and they did all that damage, and now Grandpa and Grandma like them, and you like them, and Grandma even made cookies for them. Even Patches likes them. And now that man is going to take you and the twins out for pizza, and the twins will be all excited, and they'll like him." Her words came out in a rush, and Marcie pulled Emily into her arms and sat down with the girl in her lap.

"Tom and James are nice boys, Emily, even if they did a bad thing. Their dad is in the Navy, and he's gone a lot. They don't get to see him for months at a time. That doesn't excuse their behavior, but we can help them do better from now on. Your grandfather and grandmother won't love you any less if they make new friends. And the twins and I aren't the only ones going out for pizza. Did you think we wouldn't be taking you with us?"

She gently smoothed her daughter's hair back from her face. "I know you know what it's like not to have your father around, and I know how much you love your grandparents. We're lucky we could move back here where we could be happy. We have a chance now to help Tom and James be happier than they have been. Don't you think we should try to help them?"

Emily's voice was so quiet, Marcie could barely hear her. "If you get married again, will you stop loving me?"

"I will *never* stop loving you, Emily." Marcie couldn't believe Emily had asked that question. "Why would you think I'd stop loving you?"

"Daddy didn't love me. If you married someone else, he would be my daddy, and he might not love me, either. Then you wouldn't love me anymore. And if you have a baby with him, you might love it more than me and Seth and Laurel."

"I promise you, I will always love you. And I would never marry a man who didn't love you and Seth and Laurel. I'm sorry your father left us, but that wasn't because he didn't love you. How could anyone not love you?" She tickled her daughter until Emily laughed. "I will always love you, and your grandparents will always love you. They might like Tom and James, but they will always love you. The best thing about love is that it can grow and grow, and the more you give it away, the more you have of it."

Marcie hugged Emily tightly. "I think Kyle Hughes is a nice man, and I want to see him again, but just because I go out with him a few times doesn't mean I plan to marry him anytime soon. We just met a few days ago. And if I should fall in love and decide to get married, I wouldn't marry any man unless I was sure that he loved you too. If I get married again, it will only be to a man who loves my children as much as I do. And that's a lot."

She kissed her daughter's cheek. "Now, what do you say we go see what your brother and sister are doing? We can tell them about the pizza night."

Later, after all the children were in bed, Marcie

and Jane sat in the living room, drinking the herbal tea they both liked.

Marcie was distracted, thinking about Kyle Hughes, and only realized that her aunt had spoken to her when the older woman waved a hand in front of Marcie's face.

"I'm sorry, Aunt Jane. I guess I'm not very good company right now."

Jane smiled indulgently. "That's okay, dear. I do remember what it was like to be young."

"What do you mean, Aunt Jane?"

"You can't deny you were thinking of that handsome deputy sheriff. You had a dreamy expression on your face that doesn't come from thinking about anything else but being in love."

"I'm not sure I'd say I'm in love. But I was thinking about Kyle. I admit I like him, but it's way too soon to talk about love."

"Stuff and nonsense, my dear. We don't plan love. It just happens. I saw the way he looked at you last night, and I'd say the two of you have definitely been hit by Cupid's arrow, even if it isn't February. Love doesn't take long. It sometimes happens so quickly, you hardly know what hit you."

Marcie looked at her great-aunt for a moment before she answered. "Is that what happened to you, Aunt Jane? I know Mom and Dad claim to have fallen in love at first sight, but I sure don't trust my own judgment anymore when it comes to men. Look how wrong I was about Jim."

"It wasn't that you were wrong about him, Marcie, as much as that he kept his real self hidden from everyone. He fooled all of us."

Jane stopped speaking, as if lost in memories, and then continued. "I fell in love with George Southerland the first time I saw him. He was seventeen, I was fifteen, and as soon as I laid eyes on him, I knew I wanted to marry him. We had a lot of happy years. I wouldn't trade what we had for anything."

"I just have to be so careful. It's not just me now. I have to think of the children," Marcie said.

Jane patted her on the knee. "You can't live just for your children. You should have someone to share your life with. I'm not saying you should jump into another marriage, dear. Just don't close yourself off to the possibility of love out of duty to the children. I'd say you and that handsome deputy should try dating for a while, get to know each other, and see what happens."

Marcie hugged her aunt. "How did I get so lucky to have such a wise and wonderful person as you in my life, Aunt Jane?"

Chapter Nine

Saturday dawned bright and sunny. Seth and Laurel were so excited about the upcoming pizza dinner they could hardly do anything else all day except talk about it. Emily was quiet and thoughtful. She showed no enthusiasm about dinner, which was unusual. Normally any mention of eating out was received enthusiastically by all three children.

As six o'clock drew near, Seth and Laurel were so excited, they were almost bouncing off the walls and the furniture. Marcie gave up trying to calm them down and decided to let them work off their excess energy in their own way. When they heard Kyle's car pull up in front of the house, the twins ran to the front door, flung it open wide, and tumbled out onto the porch.

"He's here! He's here! It's time for pizza!" They danced around the porch, giggling and acting goofy.

Marcie walked out onto the porch and tried to calm them down. "Hey, you two, if you don't settle down, Kyle might just change his mind and not take us out for pizza." She stood at the top of the steps to wait as Kyle got out of the car and walked up the sidewalk.

He smiled at her, and Marcie felt again the spark of awareness she experienced every time he was near. He came up the steps onto the porch, and she took in every detail of his appearance. He was wearing a long-sleeved turquoise polo shirt that really brought out the color of his eyes, and faded blue jeans that clung to his long legs. Just as she was thinking how good he looked, he echoed her thoughts.

"You look terrific, Marcie." His voice was like warm honey, and he didn't even seem to notice the twins jumping around them, as he only had eyes for her.

Once again she wore a green shirt, in a silky material that played up her coloring. Her blue jeans showed off her legs to perfection.

"I'm so hungry, I could eat a whole pizza by myself!" Seth pushed between Marcie and Kyle, and the moment was broken.

They both laughed a bit self-consciously as they looked down at the boy.

Kyle recovered quickly. "I think I know just the place to go, Seth. They serve the best pizza I've ever had, and they have ice cream for dessert. And video games." His words sent Seth and Laurel into another bout of silliness.

Marcie looked up at Kyle, asking, "Are you sure you know what you're doing? It's not too late to change your mind."

His smile left her short of breath.

"I know exactly what I'm doing, Marcie, and I have no intention of changing my mind. I plan to get to know you, and I want to be a part of your life. How could I exclude your children?" He took Seth by the hand, surprised when Laurel moved to stand on his other side and reach for his other hand. "Now, what do you say we get this show on the road?"

Marcie stepped back into the house and called Emily. When Emily reached the door, she came out onto the porch but stopped when she saw Kyle holding the twins' hands. Marcie reached behind Emily to pull the door closed. She held out her hand to her daughter and smiled. Emily took her mother's hand, and they went to Marcie's car.

When all three of the children were secure in the backseat, Marcie held out the keys to Kyle, who shook his head.

"I don't need to drive. I'm okay with sitting in the passenger seat."

Marcie couldn't stop the surprise that showed on her face. Jim had constantly criticized her driving, as he had criticized just about everything else about her. Kyle's attitude was a pleasant change. She was glad there wasn't going to be an argument about who would drive.

She was beginning to realize that being with Kyle was very different from being with her ex-husband. There was a certain tension between them, but it was more of an awareness of each other, an elemental pull between them, than an adversarial sensation. She had always felt that she wasn't good enough for Jim, that she was somehow inferior. Jim had worked hard to put her down and make her feel worthless. Kyle made her feel good about herself. Just being with him made Marcie happy.

She smiled and got into the driver's seat. He climbed in on the passenger side. They talked about a number of things on the ride to the pizza place, and not once did Kyle complain about Marcie's driving.

The restaurant wasn't crowded, and as soon as they ordered, the children ran into the game room to play video games. Kyle and Marcie chatted while they waited for their pizza. When the pizzas were delivered to the table, Marcie went to get the children. As they returned to the table, Kyle's beeper sounded.

He looked at the beeper and then excused

himself. Marcie watched him as he used his cell phone to answer his message. His expression as he walked back to the table told her everything.

"I'm sorry, Marcie. I've got to leave. That was the dispatcher. There's been a bad accident, and they need me. I told dispatch to send a car here for me. I'll have them drop me off at your place when I'm done so I can get my car, if that's all right. I'll pay for dinner, of course." He started to pull out his wallet. "I have no idea what time it will be, so if you'd rather, I can wait until tomorrow to get my car."

"No, Kyle, I'll pay. You haven't even eaten." She was disappointed that he had to leave, but Marcie didn't want him to pay for yet another dinner he wouldn't be able to eat. "And don't worry about the time. Just come get your car when you're ready."

Seth protested that he didn't want Kyle to leave, and Kyle put his hand on the boy's shoulder. "I'm sorry, Seth. We'll have to do this another time. I hate to leave, but it's my job." He dropped some bills onto the table. "My mama would have a fit if I let you pay after I invited you to dinner. Please take the money, Marcie." His smile and the look in his eyes convinced her to take the money without arguing.

They saw a patrol car pull up outside the restaurant, and Kyle turned to go. "I'm sorry, everyone. I wish I could stay." He exited the restaurant and left a silent group behind.

Seth was the first one to recover. "I'm hungry, Mom. May I eat now?"

She smiled at her son. "Of course you may, Seth. Dig in, everyone."

They were soon laughing and enjoying themselves. Marcie tried hard to mask her disappointment and keep a smile on her face for the children's sake. She wondered how often Kyle's meals were interrupted by his job.

Kyle's car was still in the yard when they got home, and still in the yard after they went to bed. When Marcie heard the dogs bark in the middle of the night, she looked out her window and saw Kyle getting into his car. Marcie watched him drive away, then sat on the window seat looking out at the stars. She wondered idly if all their dates might be jinxed because of his job.

He called on Sunday afternoon to apologize for having to leave her so abruptly the evening before. They talked and laughed easily, and Marcie realized it wouldn't take much for her to get used to talking to him on a daily basis. She liked his easy sense of humor, his laugh, the sound of his voice. She liked it that he didn't talk down to her but asked for her opinion and then listened to her answers. They made plans for him to come out to have dinner with her and the children the next Friday evening at six-thirty.

The week went by quickly, but not so quickly that Marcie hadn't caught herself thinking of Kyle at least half a dozen times a day. She found herself daydreaming several times, and even her children noticed she wasn't always paying strict attention to them when they talked to her. She felt like a teenager anticipating a date, which was a bit unsettling.

When Kyle arrived on Friday, Seth and Laurel ran to open the door and let him in. They brought him into the kitchen, and Marcie was immediately aware of him as he entered the room.

He looked quite handsome in a blue and gray sweater and jeans. His smile and easy greeting caused a flutter of awareness to skitter along her nerves. She had never felt as aware of anyone in her life as she felt about him, and she had to take a few deep breaths to calm her nerves.

He held out a bouquet of flowers, a charming mix of carnations, roses, and baby's breath. "I hope you like them. I wasn't sure if I should bring flowers, since they might not be as nice as the ones you grow yourself." He sniffed the air, which was redolent with the aromas of dinner. "Something smells great."

"We're having roast pork. It's one of the kids'

favorites. I hope you like it." She took the flowers from him, and their fingers touched, causing a feeling of intense awareness between them.

"Thank you. They're beautiful. I'll just get something to put them in. Please sit down. I hope you don't mind eating in the kitchen. The kids have got a puzzle spread out on the dining room table." She got a vase out of a cupboard and busied herself with the flowers for a few minutes. When she set the arrangement on the kitchen table, Kyle was sitting there, watching her.

He smiled, thinking how beautiful she was. She blushed as she realized he was watching her, and when she met his gaze, it seemed as if time stretched out forever. He was thinking how nice it would be to come home to this woman, this kitchen, every day.

"Will you help us work on our puzzle after supper?" Seth pulled at the arm of Kyle's sweater to get his attention.

Kyle looked down at the boy, and his heart seemed to swell in his chest. He smiled at Seth. "Sure, Seth. I'd be glad to help you with your puzzle."

Emily and Jane came into the room, and Kyle started to stand up.

Jane waved him to sit. "Please, sit down, Deputy. We aren't too formal around here."

"Thank you, ma'am, but please call me Kyle." He eased back down onto the chair, and Seth started talking to him again.

Jane began helping Marcie put supper on the table, and Emily sat down opposite Kyle. She watched him warily without saying anything.

When the food was on the table and everyone was seated, the family joined hands around the table. Kyle took Marcie's hand on his left and Seth's on his right. Marcie said grace, asking a blessing on the food and the people gathered to eat it. Kyle's thoughts drifted back to his childhood, when his own mother had insisted on saying grace before every meal. The feel of Marcie's hand in his felt so right, he didn't want to let go as she said, "Amen."

Supper with Marcie's family reminded him of family meals at his parents' house as a child. As Jane had said, they weren't too formal. The children laughed and talked but never got rowdy. They passed the platter of roast pork and bowls of vegetables and salad, and Kyle felt right at home. It was nice to be part of a lively family dinner.

After supper he sat at the dining room table, working on a huge jigsaw puzzle with Seth and Laurel and Emily, while Marcie and Jane washed the dishes. He had offered to help do the dishes, but Seth quickly reminded him of his commitment to help with the puzzle. He hadn't ever been much for putting together puzzles, but Seth and Emily were both quick and adept at finding and matching pieces. Laurel picked up a few puzzle pieces, looked at them, moved them around, then got down from her chair. She sat quietly on the floor beside her brother's chair, playing with a large stuffed rabbit dressed in a slightly tattered dress. She ignored the activity around the puzzle, content to be near her brother and sister.

Marcie walked into the dining room and stopped just inside the door. She was struck speechless by the picture of Kyle and her children enjoying themselves around the dining room table. She couldn't picture her ex-husband ever sitting with the children and working on a puzzle. It was nice to see this man taking time to do something with the tykes.

Kyle looked up, and his blue eyes sparkled with laughter. "I can't remember the last time I helped put a puzzle together."

Marcie smiled back at him. "We usually have one going. We'd be happy to let you help us again."

They talked and laughed as they put the puzzle together, and Kyle was surprised by how much he was enjoying himself. The evening had been fun, and he realized he liked Marcie's kids a lot.

When Jane came into the room and asked if anyone wanted a snack or a drink, Marcie looked at her watch and realized they had been working on the puzzle for over an hour. They had been having so much fun, she hadn't kept track of the time.

"It's getting close to bedtime, kids. Maybe Kyle will come back another time and help us finish this puzzle."

"But tomorrow's Saturday, Mom. We don't have to go to school. Can't we stay up a little longer?" Emily's question was echoed by both Seth and Laurel, who protested the idea of keeping to their normal bedtime.

"Maybe you can stay up half an hour more, but then no arguing when time's up." Marcie knew how the children felt. Bedtime on Friday nights was often pushed back because they were involved in some activity they just didn't want to abandon. As long as they went to bed at the end of the extra time without arguing, she didn't mind extending their day.

Jane left the dining room, saying she was off to bed, and Marcie, Kyle, and the children wished her a good night. The children all hugged her, then resumed their activities.

When it was time for bed, Emily and Seth went upstairs with few protests. They knew they couldn't push their mother beyond the limit she had set, and they both hugged her. Seth also hugged Kyle. Emily smiled at him but didn't offer a hug.

Kyle watched Marcie as she bent over Laurel, who had fallen asleep on the floor, her head pillowed on her stuffed rabbit. As Marcie picked up Laurel, the girl snuggled into her mother's arms, and Kyle felt a wave of tenderness for mother and child.

"Do you need help getting her upstairs?" he asked.

Marcie smiled at him and shook her head. "No, I'm fine. She's not very heavy. I'll be back down in just a few minutes if you can stay a bit longer."

"I'll be right here." He gestured to the dining room table.

"Unless you'd be more comfortable in the living room," Marcie said. "Just make yourself at home."

When she came back downstairs twenty minutes later, Kyle was sitting on the large couch in the living room, long legs stretched out in front of him, fast asleep. Marcie sat in a rocker at the far end of the room and picked up an afghan she was crocheting. She began to work on the pastel wools, glancing at the man sleeping on the couch every once in a while. Smiling to herself, she concentrated on her handiwork. The house was quiet, and Marcie enjoyed the peace, knowing the children were safely sleeping in their beds. Patches came into the room and sniffed at Kyle, then settled down next to Marcie's chair.

The only sounds in the room were the slight creaking of the rocking chair as Marcie rocked back and forth, Kyle's even breathing, and the occasional whimper of the dog as it slept.

Chapter Ten

Kyle woke about an hour later, feeling completely foolish for having fallen asleep. When he heard the noise of the rocking chair, he turned his head slowly toward the sound. He saw Marcie sitting in the rocker, the glow of the floor lamp casting golden highlights over her hair. She was looking down at an afghan spread over her lap, and he had a few minutes to study her. He liked what he saw, and he almost didn't want to let her know that he was awake. She looked up just then, and their eyes locked on one another's.

"I . . ."

"You . . ."

They both started to speak at once and then laughed together.

"You go first." Kyle sat up fully.

"I was just going to say that you must have been tired."

"And I was going to apologize for falling asleep. I guess I need to work on my dating skills." He stood up. "I can't believe I fell asleep and left you sitting there on your own."

Marcie put down the afghan and came to stand beside him. "It's all right. I rather liked knowing that you felt comfortable enough to fall asleep."

He put a finger lightly under her chin and tipped her face up to his. "I feel very comfortable here, Marcie." He leaned toward her, but just before his lips met hers, he stopped. "I just don't want to do anything to make you feel uncomfortable with me."

For her answer, she put her hands on his shoulders and pulled him toward her. He closed the short distance between them and kissed her, moving his lips gently over hers. After a brief kiss, he pulled away from her, letting the space between them grow. He stepped away from her. His hands slid down her arms until his fingertips found hers. Linking his fingers with hers, he started walking toward the front door.

"I had a really nice time tonight, Marcie. Your kids are great. I'd like to do this again." He laughed. "At least this time we were able to get through a date without being interrupted." He opened the door. "I'll call you tomorrow evening when I get off work. I've got a few ideas for our next date."

Marcie smiled at him. "Good night, Kyle." She closed the door behind him, locked it, turned off the lights, and went upstairs to bed. It had been a fun evening, and she looked forward to seeing Kyle again.

Their next date saw them taking the children to play mini golf. They laughed at one another's shots as the golf balls bounced off the blades of the windmill. When Laurel got tired and cranky, Kyle picked her up and carried her. The little girl fell asleep with her head against his shoulder, and Marcie felt a tug at her heart at the picture it made.

They went on as many dates with Marcie's children as without them. If they went to the movies, it was to a family-friendly film. Dinners were often to have pizza or burgers at places the kids picked out. Sometimes they took Tom and James Hughes with them, and both boys seemed to enjoy themselves. James liked the way Seth looked up to him as the one to ask if he had a question about the video games they played at the pizza parlor. Tom had blossomed under the teaching of Andrew and Jack Greer, and as he learned more about Jack's horses and became more involved with the family, his attitude changed drastically. Emily had lost her dislike of the boys and treated them almost like older brothers.

Since both boys were required to maintain their grades if they wanted to ride Jack's horses, their performance in school benefitted from their interaction with the Greer family.

Kyle was invited to the birthday party for Marcie's twins, and he brought presents for both of them that showed he had put a lot of thought into the purchases. The twins' birthday was a beautiful day in late October, warm and sunny, and the party was held outside. The children played games in the yard, and Marcie set up the cake and refreshments on the patio. When Seth and Laurel opened their gifts from Kyle, Marcie was a bit surprised to see things the twins had been wanting.

When she mentioned to Kyle that he must be very perceptive to have chosen the books and games that Seth and Laurel wanted, he laughed and shook his head. "I was perceptive enough to ask your Aunt Jane for a few hints."

Since late fall and winter were the slow times on the farm, with the flower beds and berry patches dormant, Marcie and Kyle were able to spend a lot of time together. The beautiful fall weather held, with warm, sunny days and cool evenings that made spending time outdoors a pleasure. On weekends they went on picnics with the children, and Marcie watched happily as Kyle and her children grew closer.

They finished several more puzzles and went for long walks and horseback rides around the farm. She pointed out areas in the fields that would bloom with thousands of daffodil bulbs in the spring and showed him the ponds that were stocked with bass, bream, and catfish. One Saturday afternoon Kyle helped Marcie and the children rake leaves; then he and the children spent as much time demolishing the piles of leaves by jumping into them as they had spent raking them.

The more time Marcie and Kyle spent together, the more time they wanted to spend together. They passed hours just talking, whether over the phone or in person. He told her about his wife and the pain he had felt when she died. He also told her about the time he'd almost proposed to a woman who was just looking for a meal ticket but had fooled him into thinking they had something special going for them.

Marcie told him about her abusive husband and the sense of worthlessness she had felt after her marriage was over. Some of their dates were interrupted when he had to leave—because as a deputy sheriff, he was often on call—but, for the most part, they were able to spend as much time together as they desired.

One Saturday afternoon Kyle came out to the farm, and they spent the afternoon baking cookies with the children. Kyle remembered afternoons like that when he and his brother had helped their mother or grandmother in the kitchen, and he thoroughly enjoyed himself. If he and the twins seemed to get flour everywhere but into the bowl where it belonged, Marcie just laughed and wiped off the white smudges.

Marcie's family welcomed Kyle into their lives. Her brother, Jack, invited him to ride his horses, and her father took him fishing in the stock ponds on the farm. Her mother found out what his favorite foods were and invited him to join in family dinners at the Greers' on Sunday afternoons. She often fixed his favorite dishes to make him feel doubly welcome.

They went dancing, and Kyle taught Marcie how to two-step. They slow danced and found themselves standing on the dance floor after the music and the other dancers had stopped. It should have been embarrassing, but Marcie felt as if she could stay in his arms forever.

Even Emily was beginning to warm up to him, and Marcie realized that Kyle was making a special effort to win Emily's trust. He had taken her and a few of her friends bowling, and he spent time working on a science project with her. He helped her with homework and often brought her and the twins small gifts, such as books and puzzles. In fact, he fit into the family so well that sometimes Marcie had to remind herself that they had only known him for a month or two. In her heart she felt as if she had known him forever.

Kyle went to Dallas to spend Thanksgiving with his parents, and he promised to call Marcie as soon as he returned. He called her on Saturday afternoon, and they made plans to have dinner together that night at Harmony Farm.

After dinner and a few hours spent playing Go Fish and Old Maid with the children, Kyle once again sat on the couch waiting as Marcie put the children to bed. When she came back downstairs, he was waiting for her at the foot of the stairway.

"I've got to be at work early, so I'll say good night now."

He kissed her gently on the lips. Stepping back, he looked into her eyes.

"Do you believe in long courtships, Marcie? Because I'm falling in love with you, and I'm hoping you'll say that you don't want a really long courtship. I know we've only known each other a short time, but I think we've got the start of something special here."

Once again Marcie thought about the fact that they hadn't known each other very long. She enjoyed his company, and they had been having a lot of fun together, and he really had been making an effort to include her children in their time together. She was torn between her life with the children and including someone else in her heart. But, looking into Kyle's eyes, she knew she wanted this man to be a part of her life.

"You're right, Kyle. We do have the start of something good. As far as the length of a courtship goes, I think we just need to take one day at a time and see how it goes. I can't rush into anything."

"There's no rush, Marcie. I just want you to know that I'm serious about you." He dropped another quick kiss onto her cheek. "Good night, Marcie. I'll call you tomorrow."

He called her on Sunday evening, and they made plans to attend a party one of his co-workers was having the following Friday. The party gave Marcie an opportunity to see Kyle in a new setting. It was a birthday party held for one of the other deputies, and it gave Marcie the chance to meet the people Kyle worked with. As the evening progressed, Marcie realized that while Kyle was never very far from her, he didn't hover, and he didn't censor her interactions with the others in attendance. By the time they left the party, Marcie had made friends with several of the women and made plans to get together with one who also had a five-year-old daughter, so the children could play together.

The trip back to Marcie's was full of talk about the party and plans for the future. They were planning a trip to Branson, Missouri, to look at the

Christmas lights. The twins and Emily had already told their mother that they wanted Kyle to help them put up their Christmas tree, and they talked about when they would do that. Kyle kissed her good night at her door and waited until he heard her lock the door behind her before turning to walk to his car. Life was wonderful, he thought as he drove away from Harmony Farm.

The month of December passed much as the preceding three, with the addition of the excitement over the holidays added to the mix. Kyle and Marcie spent as much time together as possible. He helped her shop for Christmas presents for the children and her family. One Saturday afternoon they put up the tree and decorations. It was ten days until Christmas, and the kids' excitement was palpable. By the time bedtime rolled around, Laurel was almost asleep, and even Seth was winding down.

Kyle watched as Marcie shepherded the children up the stairs. Seth turned for one last look at the Christmas tree. "This is going to be the best Christmas ever, isn't it, Mom?"

Marcie smiled at her son. "It is going to be special, Seth, but right now let's get you and your sisters into bed." Once the children were tucked in, Marcie went downstairs to find Kyle standing by the Christmas tree. He turned as she came up behind him and slipped her arms around his waist.

Pulling her close, he led her to the couch. They sat down, and Marcie eased back into his arms.

"Did you get the kids settled down? I can't believe how much energy Seth always has. He never seems to slow down."

"Even Seth was ready for bed. He does seem to have more energy than any other child I've ever met." It felt good to be able to lean against Kyle and enjoy the warmth of his body next to hers.

They sat together for several minutes without speaking, just enjoying the sight of the Christmas tree with its twinkling lights. Marcie roused herself enough to ask if Kyle wanted anything to eat or drink, and he hugged her just a bit more tightly.

"Sitting here like this, holding you, I feel as if I've got everything I need right now." He realized he was content to simply sit and hold the woman who was becoming such an important part of his life. "That's not to say that this is all I'll ever want, but right now, this feels nice." He tipped her face up toward his and kissed her. "But as nice as this is, Marcie, I've got to work tomorrow, so I think I'd better get going."

They walked to the front door, holding hands. Kyle picked up his coat and put it on. He stuck his hands into his coat pockets and smiled. "There is one more thing, Marcie. Before I go, I have something for you." He pulled a small box from his coat pocket and held it out to her.

She stared at him, unable to move. She looked at the blue velvet ring box, feeling totally dazed as he pressed the box into her hand. She fumbled with the lid, and when she saw the ring inside, she gasped in shock.

The ring was an ornate gold filigree band set with the largest emerald Marcie had ever seen. The gem was flanked by two large round diamonds, either one of which would have been more than adequate by itself. She looked up at him in wonder, and when he saw the tears start to run down her cheeks, he felt his heart stop. He didn't know what he would do if she said no. He felt as if he were standing on the edge of a precipice, unsure of his footing. It would be a long drop if he tumbled over the edge.

Marcie finally found her voice, and her words were those he longed to hear.

"Oh, Kyle, it's beautiful. Yes, I'll marry you." Tears were flowing freely down her cheeks, and he gathered her into a tender embrace.

Kyle felt his heart resume its normal rhythm. "Don't cry, Marcie. Please, don't cry." He wiped her tears away with his thumbs, then gently touched his lips to her brow.

"I'm sorry, Kyle. It's just that I am so happy."

He kissed her again, not quite so gently. "I was thinking maybe we could get married in the spring. Perhaps in April or May, when the flowers will be in bloom."

She looked up at him. "That isn't much time, Kyle. How big a wedding are you planning? What about your family? I haven't even met your family, except Janie and the boys."

"You know that my parents and one grandmother live in Dallas, and they will love you just as much as I do. They'll be thrilled to come here anytime to meet you. I don't care if it's a big wedding, a small wedding, or a quick trip to the nearest justice of the peace." He began kissing her again. "I even thought we might have the ceremony at the farm, since it was because of your flowers that we met in the first place. We'll have the wedding you want, Marcie. As long as you say, 'I do,' I'll be happy."

"We haven't known each other very long. Are we moving too fast?" She couldn't help the doubts that were starting to creep into her mind, and he heard it in the tone of her voice. She looked down at the ring, which still rested in its box. "We haven't talked about where we'd live. Do you want us to move in with you, or will you be okay living here? There are so many things we haven't talked about."

"Marcie, look at me." He tipped her chin up. "I love you. I never really thought I would feel this way again. When my wife died, I thought I'd spend the rest of my life alone. I've found something with you that goes so far beyond what I ever dreamed of having. When I was married before, I was barely more than a kid. If my wife had lived, I would still be married to her now. I believe in long-term commitments. And I'm old enough now to know that what we have is special, and it isn't going to go away. I felt sparks fly between us the first time I saw you in the sheriff's department, and they haven't stopped since. The last few months, we've spent enough time together for me to realize that I want to spend the rest of my life with you and your children."

He took the ring box from her, took out the ring, and slipped it onto her finger. "When I told my parents and grandmother about you over Thanksgiving, my grandmother gave me this ring. It belonged to her mother, and it's been in her jewelry box for years." He drew Marcie to him and kissed her. "Nana said it's time it was worn by a beautiful woman again. She can't wait to see you wearing it.

"I want to come home to you every night, to eat breakfast with you every morning, to see you crocheting afghans for our babies. As for where we live, I would be glad to live here. It's beautiful here, and it's where you and the kids call home. I can't ask you to uproot them and move to town."

She looked up at him and saw something in his eyes that took her breath away.

"Yes, Marcie, I want to have children with you. I love you, and I want children. I'm thirty-two. I don't want to wait too long to start adding to our family." He laughed and kissed her again. "But don't make me wait for summer, please. Life is too short to waste."

He brought her hand to his lips and placed a kiss on her palm. He curled her fingers over her palm and kissed her knuckle, next to the emerald ring. "Good night, Marcie. I'll see you tomorrow. I'll come by in the evening, if that's all right with you."

He felt lighthearted as he walked to his car.

Chapter Eleven

In the morning, Jane was the first one downstairs. When Marcie came down and started fixing pancakes for the children, it didn't take long for Jane to notice the ring.

"Oh, my. Is that an engagement ring? I knew you and Kyle were right for each other. Have you set a date?" She hugged Marcie tightly. "I'm so happy for you, dear. I've seen your happiness grow the last few months, and you and Kyle both deserve to be happy."

"We talked about the possibility of a spring wedding. That's only a few months away. I don't know if that will be enough time." Just as Marcie finished saying it, Emily came into the kitchen. Emily sat at the table, and Marcie kissed her on the cheek.

"Enough time for what, Mom?"

Marcie sat next to her daughter. "Last night Kyle asked me to marry him, sweetheart. I said yes. We were thinking about maybe having the wedding here in the spring."

Emily looked down at her mother's hand as Marcie reached out to take her daughter's hands in hers. Emily didn't say anything about the ring on her mother's finger, but she reached out to touch it.

"I hope you like Kyle enough to let him be part of our family, Emily. I'm sure we can all be happy together. I told you I wouldn't marry anyone who didn't love you and the twins, and I'm sure Kyle loves you."

The twins came into the room then, and Emily didn't reply. As they ate breakfast, Marcie noticed that Emily seemed to be her usual cheerful self, so she didn't let herself worry over her eldest's reaction to the news. The twins accepted the announcement happily, declaring that they were glad to be getting Kyle for their new father. It hadn't taken long for Kyle to win their support, and they were quite vocal in their support of the plan.

The trip to church that morning was full of laughter, and as they settled into their pew for the service, Marcie had a hard time trying to get the children to be quiet. When her parents came in and sat with them, her mother caught on to the twins' excitement right away, and it was only a few minutes before they explained that they were getting a new father in a few months. Sharon Greer could hardly wait until the service was over to question Marcie, and when she caught sight of the engagement ring, she was hard-pressed to keep from exclaiming out loud.

As soon as the final "Amen" was said, Sharon was able to give voice to the questions that had been threatening to burst out during the service.

Realizing that they were quickly becoming a focal point for all the parishioners who had not yet left the chapel, Marcie felt embarrassed and announced that she would answer all of her mother's questions when they got outside. The few minutes it took to leave the building, say hello to friends, and thank the pastor for his words were too long for Sharon but way too short for Marcie.

As soon as they were out on the sidewalk, Sharon grabbed Marcie into a hug and began questioning her. "When did Kyle give you that beautiful ring? Where did he get it? How did Emily take the news? When is the wedding? Oh, Marcie, I'm so happy for you! This is so exciting!"

"Mom, please, slow down." Marcie noticed that they were still the center of attention as people made their way to their cars. She began walking toward her own car, drawing her mother along with her. "Kyle gave me the ring last night. It was his great-grandmother's, and his grandmother gave it to him when he told his family he was going to ask me to marry him. We're thinking about getting married on the farm in the spring."

"That would be beautiful. We could set up a gazebo facing the flower beds. Oh, I don't know, there's so much to do to plan a wedding. What about Kyle's family? You haven't even met his parents yet."

"We've decided we want a small wedding, Mom. Just family and close friends. Kyle said his parents and grandmother will be glad to come up from Dallas to meet me, and we're going to work that out the next time we get together. His brother is supposed to be home on leave by Christmas, and Kyle is going to ask him if he can get home again in the spring to be his best man."

Andrew Greer spoke up for the first time. "Well, Marcie, it looks as if there was a silver lining to the damage those Hughes boys did. You met a fine man, and your brother and I have ended up with first-class help. Tom has been working with Jack and has turned into a fine hand. He really enjoys working with the horses and shows a great deal of promise. He's turning into quite a good rider. And James is a joy to have around. He reminds me of you when you were younger. He's eager to learn everything he can about the nursery business, and he's smart as can be."

"You're right about that, Dad." She hugged her

father and kissed him on the cheek. "I'm glad every-thing turned out the way it has."

Lunch at the Greers' home was a festive affair, with everyone offering suggestions for the wedding. It was decided that Emily and Laurel could be flower girls, Seth would carry the pillow bearing the rings down the aisle, and Nancy would be Marcie's maid of honor.

She was laughing when she said, "We really only talked about getting married, not about any of the practical matters involved. When we get together again, we'll go over everything."

Sharon began jotting down everyone's suggestions on a sheet of paper. "We might as well start making notes. Oh, this is wonderful. I couldn't think of a better man for you, Marcie. We'll all be proud to welcome Kyle into the family."

They began to clear the lunch dishes, and Marcie's mother refused to let her help. She urged Marcie to sit and enjoy her status as a newly engaged woman, which prompted Marcie to remain at the table, smiling as she thought about marrying Kyle. Her seeming inattention to the conversation brought a lot of teasing from her family, but Marcie didn't mind.

She was still smiling when the phone rang and her father answered it. As she heard what he said, her smile slipped. Three words had ripped apart her world .

"Kyle's been shot?" Andrew's voice cut through the laughter in the room. "Yes, Ben, I'll bring her to the hospital right away. Have you notified his sister-in-law?" He looked at Marcie as she sat white-faced at the table. "We'll be there directly."

Andrew hung up the phone and walked around the table to Marcie. "I'm sorry, honey. That was Ben Jamison. There was an incident at the pharmacy in town. Kyle's been shot. I'll take you to the hospital. Ben didn't have any details, so I don't know how bad it is."

He helped her up from her chair, steadying her when she swayed slightly. Everyone except Marcie began talking at once, asking questions Andrew Greer couldn't answer. Marcie was too numb to ask anything. All she could think was that she had just found Kyle, and now he was going to die. She clung to her father's arm as he led her out of the house and to his car.

Chapter Twelve

When they arrived at the hospital, Kyle was in surgery. He had been shot three times, and his condition was critical. Because Marcie was not related to him, no one would give her specific information. Ben Jamison met them in the waiting area outside the operating room and told them what he knew.

Kyle had gone into the local Walgreens to make a purchase and interrupted an attempted robbery. One robber had shot him as Kyle tried to talk to him. He hadn't been wearing a bulletproof vest and had taken one slug in the arm, one in the chest, and one in the stomach. The arm wound was considered minor.

Marcie flinched at hearing Sheriff Jamison

describe a gunshot wound as "minor." Her father gripped her arm tightly and helped her sit down.

Ben Jamison stood in front of her, and the worry in his face mirrored her own. "I'm sorry, Marcie. I didn't mean to upset you or sound uncaring, but the wound in Kyle's arm is really not the problem. It's the others we have to worry about. But Kyle is strong, and the paramedics got him here fast. The surgeon on duty is a good one."

All Marcie could think to do was pray. She wasn't sure how long she sat there praying for Kyle. She wasn't aware of her mother's coming into the waiting room until Sharon Greer sat next to her and put her arm around Marcie's shoulders. She looked into her mother's eyes and couldn't hold in the tears she had been fighting.

"What will I do if he doesn't make it? Oh, Mom, how could this have happened?" She sobbed against her mother's shoulder as the older woman held her.

Sharon Greer stroked her daughter's cheek. "Kyle is strong, dear, and he has a lot to live for. I'm sure he'll make it. Jack and Nancy are going to stay at your place tonight, and they'll help Jane get the children to school in the morning. Your father and I will stay here with you." She touched Marcie gently, smoothing the hair back from her face.

It was nearly three more hours before the doors

opened and the surgeon came into the waiting room. Sheriff Jamison stood up and met the doctor in the middle of the room.

"Your deputy is in grave condition, Ben. I've repaired all the damage I could. He's young, strong, and in good shape, so that's a plus. The next forty-eight hours or so will tell." The doctor hesitated, then continued. "In addition to the gunshot wounds, it seems he was struck in the head. I don't know what weapon was used, but he may have a concussion. It worries me a bit, coming on top of the other wounds and the anesthesia. Have you contacted his family?"

"His sister-in-law and her two boys are out of town for the weekend. I've put in a call to them and to his parents in Dallas. They should be here soon." He nodded toward Marcie. "His fiancée is here, Doctor. Is there any chance she can see him?"

The doctor looked over at Marcie and shook his head. "Not yet, I'm afraid. He's in the recovery room. I'll leave orders that she be allowed to see him as soon as he's moved out of recovery. He'll be in the ICU, and usually only family would be allowed in, but I'll make an exception in this case, since he'll be the only patient in ICU." The doctor smiled at Marcie. "With a fiancée as pretty as you, he's got a lot to live for, and I intend to keep him alive. You need to get some rest and try not to worry too much. It won't help him if you get run-down."

The sheriff shook hands with the surgeon and turned to Marcie as the doctor left the waiting room. "The doctor's right. You should go home and get some rest, Marcie."

"I'm staying right here, Ben. I won't go home until I see Kyle."

He looked as if he might insist she leave, but he nodded and said, "I'll be right back." He walked toward the nurses' station, and a few minutes later he came back with pillows and blankets. He set them on the couch where Marcie sat with her mother. "If you're going to stay, you might as well be more comfortable. Please, try to lie down and rest." He sat down in one of the chairs. His face looked tired, and Marcie thought how lucky Kyle was to have a friend and boss like Ben Jamison.

She fell asleep around midnight and awakened to the sound of voices. She sat up slowly, not realizing for a second why she was sleeping on an unfamiliar couch. When realization hit, she stood up to see Ben talking to three strangers. He led them over to her and introduced them.

"Marcie, these are Kyle's parents, Charles and Betty Hughes, and his grandmother, Sallie Lassiter." He gestured to Marcie and her parents. "And this is Marcie Connor, Kyle's fiancée, and her parents, Sharon and Andrew Greer."

Kyle's mother swept Marcie into her arms, hugging her tightly. "I am so glad to meet you, Marcie, although I certainly never thought it would be under these circumstances. Kyle has told us so much about you, and I'm so grateful he has you in his life now." She stepped back and looked at Marcie carefully. "You are just as beautiful as he said you were. Have you been able to see him yet?"

Marcie couldn't believe Kyle's mother could call her beautiful. She knew how she must look, with her hair and clothes disheveled from her hours of waiting. She shook her head. "We're still waiting for word from the nurses. The doctor said he would have someone notify us as soon as Kyle is moved from recovery into the ICU."

A sound from the older woman brought Marcie's attention to Kyle's grandmother. "Please, won't you sit here with me?" Marcie gently helped the woman to the couch. As they sat together, Kyle's grandmother took Marcie's left hand between her own hands. She held Marcie's hand lightly.

"You may call me Nana, as Kyle does, or Sallie if you like. I have waited a long time for my grandson to fall in love and get married again. He is going to be all right, Marcie. I'll see you walk down the aisle." She patted Marcie's hand. "Please, don't worry, my dear. I know he will be all right."

Kyle's mother sat on the other side of Marcie. "My mother's maiden name is Donovan, Marcie, and she has been blessed with what the Irish call 'second sight.' She has assured us that she has seen you walking down the aisle to meet Kyle. I've never known her to be wrong when she 'sees' something."

Marcie smiled at Kyle's mother. "I certainly hope you're right." Before she could say anything else, a nurse came into the waiting room.

"We've moved Mr. Hughes into the ICU. He's come out of the anesthesia, but he isn't awake. We kept him in the recovery room a bit longer than normal because of the possibility of concussion. The doctor said his fiancée was here. He said to let you in to see Mr. Hughes."

Marcie stood up. "I'm his fiancée, but his parents and grandmother are here now too. They should be the first to see him."

"Two people can go in at a time to see him. I'll let you decide which two go in first." The nurse turned and walked back through the doorway.

Betty Hughes took Marcie by the hand. "I think Marcie and I will go in to him first, if that's all right with everyone else."

Her husband kissed her on the cheek. "Of course, my dear. You and Marcie go ahead."

Sallie Lassiter also nodded her assent. "I'm sure hearing Marcie's voice will do Kyle a world of good." She patted Marcie on the arm. "Please give

Kyle my love, and don't worry. Everything will be just fine."

Marcie and Betty walked into the ICU, and the nurse who had spoken to them directed them to the cubicle where Kyle was. He lay on the bed, barely alive, hooked up by tubes to a machine that helped him breathe, an IV line that slowly dripped fluid into his arm, and wires to monitor his vital signs.

Marcie felt her legs turn to rubber as she stood next to the bed. Kyle looked so pale and wan. His head was partially shaved, and one eye was blackened. The whole left side of his face was bruised and scraped.

Betty Hughes took Marcie by the arm. She stepped to the bed and began speaking to Kyle. "Hello, Kyle. It's Mom. Marcie is here with me, and your father and grandmother are out in the waiting room. They'll be in later to talk to you." She squeezed his hand. "You were right, Kyle. Marcie is beautiful, and we all love her already. Your grandmother said to tell you she loves you, and she's planning to dance with you at your wedding."

Marcie watched the Kyle's mother, wondering how she could be so strong and talk to her son as if he weren't lying in an intensive-care unit barely clinging to life. She didn't think she could do it, and she felt a sob building in her chest. It took all the strength she had to keep from giving in to the hysteria she felt bubbling up. Trying not to focus on the tubes going into his mouth and nose, Marcie moved closer to the bed. She took Kyle's hand in hers and couldn't help the gasp that escaped her lips. His hand was so cold. She rubbed it gently between her fingers.

"Hello, Kyle." She was struggling to keep the tears that stung her eyes from falling. Kyle's mother gripped Marcie's arm tightly. Marcie took a deep breath and bent and started speaking again, her voice unwavering. "I love you, Kyle. I know that you love me too. We can get through this together. I'll be right here when you wake up. You need to rest now, and your mother and I can only stay a few minutes longer. We'll be back soon. I like your parents and your grandmother. They're as nice as you said they were."

Kyle heard and recognized her voice. Marcie. The woman he loved and planned to marry. But he couldn't think. He was in too much pain.

Betty Hughes spoke to her son again. "Your father and grandmother will be in to see you soon, Kyle. Then Marcie and I will be back. Rest now, son. I love you." She stepped away from the bed and took Marcie's hand, and the two women left the cubicle.

They updated the others in the waiting room

on their visit, and Ben Jamison said he needed to leave. He was on his way to his office to monitor developments in the case. Marcie and Kyle's fathers shook Ben's hand and thanked him for being there. He hugged Marcie before he left, and his last words were, "I'll dance with you at your wedding, young lady, if I can get you out of Kyle's arms long enough." He smiled at her and walked away.

Marcie dropped onto the couch, exhausted but too keyed up to sleep.

Kyle's grandmother sat beside her, putting her arms around the younger woman's shoulders and drawing her close. "You need to rest, my dear. I know you don't want to, but it won't do Kyle any good if you don't take care of yourself." She pulled the blanket around Marcie. Smoothing Marcie's hair back from her face, Sallie began talking softly, telling her stories about Kyle's childhood. Marcie felt herself relax against the older woman and fell asleep against her shoulder in the middle of a story about Kyle's first pony.

As Kyle's grandmother spoke to Marcie, Kyle lay in the bed in the ICU. Everything was fuzzy in his mind. His head hurt, and trying to think made the pain worse.

All of a sudden he thought of his grandmother. He remembered when his grandparents had bought him a pony. He had been about five or six, and the pony was a sassy Shetland named Scout. He hadn't thought about that pony for years, but suddenly he could see it as clearly as if someone were showing him a picture. He could almost hear his grandmother, and he wondered if she was close by. He gave in to his body's need for sleep, and his thoughts slipped away like dried leaves on an autumn wind.

When Marcie woke up, it was almost eight o'clock in the morning. The waiting room was quiet, and the rest of the group was still sleeping. She eased off the couch and stretched out the aches she had from sleeping on the couch.

A nurse came into the waiting room and spoke quietly to Marcie, trying not to wake the others. She told Marcie that Kyle had passed a quiet, restful night, and while he was not awake at the moment, he had awakened during the night. She also said the doctor had been in and examined him and was pleased with his progress. She allowed Marcie into the ICU for a minute or two, even though visiting hours didn't start for two hours.

As everyone woke up, the first thing they wondered was whether Kyle had awakened. Marcie relayed what the nurse had told her and her own observations that he was resting peacefully, and they were all glad to hear the news. They decided to go to the hospital cafeteria for breakfast. None of them felt like eating, but they all knew they had to. It was a sober but hopeful group that trooped back into the waiting room a short time later.

Chapter Thirteen

Marcie spent her allotted time with Kyle the next morning and watched him carefully for signs that he knew she was there. When she told him she loved him and squeezed his hand, this time he squeezed back. It was barely noticeable, but, even as slight as it was, the gesture meant Kyle was listening to her, that he was aware she was there with him. When her ten minutes were up, Marcie returned to the waiting room with a renewed spirit. She gave a small prayer of thanks that Kyle had responded to her touch, and she was smiling as she joined their family members.

The others were awake and discussing breakfast when Marcie joined them. Her report of Kyle's restful night and the fact that he had squeezed her

136

hand as she spoke to him brought smiles all around. They decided to go to Harmony Farm to eat and change so they could come back in time for the next visiting period, which would be at ten o'clock.

Jane, Nancy, and Jack had gotten the children off to school, and Nancy and Jack had gone home to take care of their horses. Jane quickly began preparations for breakfast as Marcie showered and changed. The rest of the two families had gone to Andrew and Sharon's house. Kyle's family had spoken of finding a motel room, but the Greers insisted there was no need of motels when they had plenty of rooms.

The group that returned to the hospital exhausted from their vigil of the night before was refreshed in body and spirit. They were able to smile as they sat in the waiting room. Talking about wedding plans helped pass the time, and Marcie was more than happy to insist that Kyle's family should take the next visit, since she had seen him earlier that morning. Janie Hughes arrived and joined the group in the waiting room. She had sent her boys to school that morning and planned to pick them up afterward and bring them to the hospital.

Kyle's mother and father went in to see him, and when they came out, they reported that he had opened his eyes for a few minutes. He had tried to speak to them but couldn't because of the tube down his throat, but he was aware of their visit.

The news further cheered Marcie, and she began to let herself dream of walking down the aisle with Kyle. The thought of seeing him in only a few hours kept her spirits up, and she gave thanks that he seemed to be on the mend.

It was just before the ten o'clock visit when Marcie heard a voice over the loudspeaker announcing a code in the ICU. The call for Kyle's doctor to report to the unit caused her heart to almost stop. She felt cold all over and began praying. She was grateful for Kyle's parents, who sat next to her, helping her remain strong.

One of the nurses came out to see them. "I thought I'd better come out and talk to you. We had another patient brought in to the ICU. He has the same doctor as Mr. Hughes. Don't worry—Mr. Hughes is doing fine."

The group in the waiting room relaxed and thanked her for her news.

By the next visit, Marcie's parents had returned, and she stayed with them while Kyle's parents visited him. The rest of the day was spent in short visits with Kyle and sitting and waiting as the hours crawled by.

Ben came by to tell them that the man who shot Kyle had been captured. The store's security camera had captured the incident on tape. They had run the tape on the news, and a tip had come in that led to the capture of one suspect. The other perpetrator was sure to be caught soon. It had been the second man who had struck Kyle in the head, and the security cameras had gotten that on tape as well. The general feeling in town was that whoever had done this would be caught soon.

Marcie ate the lunch her father brought, barely tasting the food but knowing she needed to eat to keep up her strength. Janie and Tom went in to see Kyle for the four o'clock visit, and Janie was visibly shaken when they came out. "Kyle has always been so strong. I can't bear to see him like this." She began to cry, and Kyle's grandmother handed her a tissue.

"Now, Janie, you just stop crying right now. Kyle will be fine." She took Janie by the shoulders and led her to the couch. Her practical, no-nonsense attitude brooked no argument, and Janie settled down with her, without protest.

Marcie and her parents went home to spend some time with her children, then returned to the hospital. Kyle's parents and grandmother took Janie and the boys out for supper, returning in time for the eight o'clock visit.

They stayed at the hospital until the last visit was allowed at 10:00 P.M., then repeated the previous evening's return to Harmony Farm. Janie offered to have them come stay with her, but as their things were already at Harmony Farm, it was decided that they would continue to stay there.

Walking into the ICU at eight the next morning, Marcie was thrilled to see that Kyle's eyes were open as she approached his bed. He still had the tubes in his mouth and nose, but the nurse came by to say that the doctor planned to remove them later that morning.

He tried to talk to Marcie, but the nurse quickly shushed him. "Don't try to talk yet, Mr. Hughes. After the tubes are removed, you can talk. Right now you need to let everyone else do the talking. And if you're really good, we'll move you downstairs into a regular room in a few days." She smiled at him, made a few notes on his chart, and left the cubicle.

The doctor came in between the ten o'clock and noon visits and removed the tubes from Kyle's nose and throat. His mother and father were the first to visit him after the doctor left, and he tried to talk to his mother, but his throat was so sore from the tube that he couldn't speak. He was only able to get out one word—*Marcie*—and his mother assured him that Marcie would be in to visit him soon.

Kyle shook his head, an action he soon regretted, and closed his eyes. He was frustrated that he couldn't speak. His mother was talking about how much the family liked Marcie. He wanted to make them understand, but how? How could he tell them he had changed his mind about marrying the woman he loved?

He knew, as surely as he knew he was lying in a hospital bed, that it wouldn't be fair to ask Marcie to marry him. How could he ask her to sign on for a lifetime of not knowing if he would come home from work every day? He could get shot again, and the next time he might not survive. It wouldn't be right to ask Marcie to marry him and then make her a widow. He loved her, but he couldn't marry her. And he couldn't give up his job, not even for Marcie. His job was part of who he was.

He had always wanted to be a cop, ever since he could remember, and the job with the sheriff's department was his dream come true. He'd worked as a cop in Dallas, and when he came out to Arkansas to visit Tom and Janie, who had moved here to live near her parents, he'd applied for the job with the sheriff's department. Until he'd been shot a few days ago, the job here had seemed safer than working in the city.

He slept through the next visit, and Janie and James came to see him at the one after that. Marcie didn't come in again that afternoon, and his mother told him she had gone home to spend some time with her children.

He didn't know if he could face her again. How could he tell her he couldn't marry her? She had become so important to him in such a short time. She was the most beautiful woman he had ever known, both inside and out, and he was going to have to tell her he couldn't marry her.

Charles Hughes and Sallie Lassiter visited Kyle at six o'clock, and Sallie noticed that when they mentioned Marcie, Kyle seemed to withdraw from them. She saw the sadness that lingered in his eyes and asked her son to step out so she could speak to her grandson alone.

After Charles left, Sallie took Kyle's hand in hers. "What's bothering you, Kyle? I know something's wrong, and I'd like to help if I can."

Kyle closed his eyes, not wanting to meet his grandmother's piercing blue gaze. She had always been able to read him so well; she saw things even his mother missed. He opened his eyes and looked up at his beloved grandmother. How could he tell her what he was thinking?

Sallie touched him gently on the right cheek, the unbruised side of his face. "You're thinking of Marcie, aren't you? And if I don't miss my guess, you're wondering if you should try to discourage her from marrying you."

He would have laughed if he could have. Her hunch was exactly right. "How did you know?" He rasped out the words.

"Ah, Kyle. You know I can read you like a book. I've always known when you were hurting, and

I've felt your sadness and your happiness. You're worried that if you ask Marcie to marry you and something like this happens again, you might not make it."

"Yes," he answered. "What if I died? She'd be alone, and I can't take that chance. I lost Ella, and I know how it felt. I can't ask Marcie to go through that."

The nurse came by to remind them that visiting hours were over. "And you need to be resting, Mr. Hughes. We have to get you out of here and into a regular room, so that beautiful fiancée of yours can spend more time with you." She smiled at them both, not seeing the flash of pain in Kyle's eyes.

Sallie kissed him gently on the cheek. "I'll be back later, Kyle. Please, don't say anything to Marcie or anyone else. We'll talk about this later." She left the ICU and paused in the hallway before walking through the doors into the waiting room.

Marcie was standing by a window, looking out without really seeing what was out there. She didn't turn as Sallie approached her. Sallie took her by the arm. "Would you like to walk with me for a few minutes, Marcie? I need to move around and get out of this waiting room." She didn't wait for Marcie to answer but started walking away from the others. "We'll be back in a few minutes."

They headed down the hall to the elevator and took it to the ground floor. Sallie led Marcie outside, and they walked for a few minutes without speaking. Sallie wondered what would happen to this woman if Kyle decided not to marry her. Marcie Connor was everything Sallie wanted for her elder grandson, and she wasn't about to let Kyle walk away from her.

She took a deep breath and let it out slowly. "It's a lovely day today, my dear. Thank you for coming out with me. I just couldn't sit in that waiting room a minute longer." She sat on one of the benches placed in the winter-barren gardens surrounding the hospital. "I'll be happy when spring gets here and your gardens are blooming. I want to visit then to see it."

"I'd love to have you visit for as long as you want. Kyle and I plan to live in my house, and we have plenty of room." Marcie was sure Kyle would be happy to have his grandmother come to visit. Sallie Lassiter was such a big part of his life, and Marcie knew her children would love the older woman. They could use an extra grandmother, and she was sure Sallie and Betty would both easily fill that role.

"I would be delighted to come and stay with you, Marcie. I love both my grandsons, and I'm happy that Kyle has found someone to love who loves him." She slanted Marcie a look. "I had almost given up hope of seeing him marry again. I just hope this hasn't given you reason to change your mind." She gestured toward the hospital. "A lot of women might not want to marry a man whose job can be so dangerous."

"I hadn't planned on ever marrying again," Marcie replied. "And I'm afraid Kyle and I didn't hit it off too well when we first met. Did he tell you about that?" When Sallie smiled and nodded, Marcie continued. "My first husband was a car salesman. He had a nice, safe job, but he also had a temper and a tendency to blame me for everything that he perceived as wrong." She took a deep breath. "I'd marry Kyle today if I could. I don't believe in borrowing worry about tomorrow, but I also know I'm strong enough to deal with whatever comes along in the future. If, for some reason, our future together is short, I'll deal with it when the time comes. Right now, I'm ready to grab this chance for happiness."

She looked Sallie in the eye. "I know something could happen to Kyle. His job is dangerous. I won't tell you that I'll never worry about him when he goes to work. I'll simply pray for his safety and wait for him to come home. It's what he does, who he is. I won't ask him to change jobs, to give up doing what he loves to do." She smiled at Sallie. "I have a tendency to bake when I'm upset. I guess I'll keep the cookie jars full."

Sallie leaned close and hugged Marcie tightly. "I'm so glad to hear you say that, Marcie. Now, what do you say we go back in and see if it's time to visit Kyle?" She was right. This was the woman her grandson needed in his life, even if he was in too much pain to think clearly at the moment. And she didn't intend to let him throw away this chance for happiness.

Chapter Fourteen

For several more days they kept to the same routine. They visited Kyle in the ICU, watching him become stronger day by day. At night they went to Harmony Farm to eat and sleep. And as the days passed, Marcie grew closer to Kyle's parents and grandmother. That lady had kept her own counsel, not saying a word to anyone about Kyle's declaration that he couldn't marry Marcie. Fortunately, Kyle himself had not said anything to anyone else.

The day came that Kyle was moved out of the ICU into a regular room, and Emily, Seth, and Laurel wanted to visit him after school. They asked Marcie to stop on the way to the hospital to buy him some get-well balloons and proudly held the strings as they walked into his room. Marcie tied

147

the strings to the foot of the bed, and they bobbed gently, a bright rainbow of color.

Kyle couldn't meet Marcie's eyes as she and the children came into the room. He thanked the children for the balloons, assured them that he was going to be out of the hospital soon, and felt like the world's biggest fraud as he listened to the twins talking about how great it was going to be to have him for their father. His heart lay heavy in his chest as he thought about telling Marcie he couldn't marry her. But how could he ever put her through this as his wife?

Emily hung back a bit and seemed to be watching him warily. He wondered what she was thinking, but she was harder to read than the twins. They were so open, so loving, and so vocal, he had no doubts about what they were thinking. They wanted to know all about the shooting, and he smiled as Marcie tried to divert their attention. His face hurt when he smiled, reminding him that he must look like something out of a horror movie. Seth was fascinated by his black eye and bruises, commenting on the range of colors around his eye.

When it was time for them to leave, Emily walked back to his bed as her mother, sister, and brother walked out the door. She spoke so quietly, he almost missed her words.

"Do you think this happened because I didn't

want you to date my mom? Or because I didn't like you?" She was trying to be brave and not cry.

Kyle felt his as if his heart would break. "No, Emily, that's not why this happened." He held out his hand to her, and she put her small hand in his. "I was at the scene of an attempted robbery, and the people who did this would have hurt any officer who was there. Those two gunmen were responsible, no one else."

She squeezed his hand. "I'm glad you're going to be okay." She opened her mouth to say something else just as Marcie stepped back into the room and called her name. "I've got to go. Bye, Kyle."

He met Marcie's eyes across the room, and time seemed to stop. They stared at each other for a long moment, and then someone spoke to Marcie from outside the room, and she turned, breaking the spell. They hadn't been alone together, and he didn't know when he would be able to tell her he couldn't marry her. He felt as if his heart were being ripped in two. He loved her, and he wanted her, but he wanted to spare her from the possibility of losing him if he died in the line of duty. That possibility had been brought home very forcefully, and he couldn't get past it.

His grandmother entered the room, greeting him with a kiss on the cheek. "You're looking very well today, Kyle. And look at these balloons. Marcie and the children are good for you."

He held her gaze without flinching. "I won't change my mind, Nana."

"Do you really think you can close your heart to her, Kyle? I've seen the way you look at her, and I listened to you at Thanksgiving when you spoke of her. Can you really give up this chance for love? I know what you are afraid of, but what are the odds that something like this will happen again? You could be giving up years of happiness and love, giving up your chance to have a family, for nothing. There are no guarantees in life. We just have to make the most of the time we have."

He didn't answer her. He didn't know what to say except what he had already said.

"If you can look me in the eye and tell me you don't love Marcie, I'll accept what you say." She pulled a chair up next to the bed.

He couldn't do it, and she knew she was right.

"We all have to face the fact that we are not immortal, my dear. But if we live in fear of loss, in fear of dying, we are not really living. Marcie accepts the fact that your job is a big part of who you are. She doesn't want to change you, and she doesn't expect you to change for her. She loves you for who you are, an honorable man who is trying to make a difference in the world."

"She's been through a lot, Nana. Before this

happened, I hadn't really given much thought to the fact that it could. I guess I'd gotten complacent, thinking it was safe here. I wasn't even wearing a bulletproof vest. I always wore one in Dallas. It didn't seem necessary here."

"Being shot isn't the only danger in life, Kyle. People die every day in auto accidents, from illnesses, and for a variety of reasons. Life is for living, not cowering and worrying about what might happen." She looked at her watch. "Well, I've had my say. I asked Betty and Charles for fifteen minutes alone with you, my time is up, and they'll be here any second. Please, think about what I've said."

His parents came into the room, and they were soon talking and laughing. He felt his grandmother's eyes on him, but they had no chance to speak privately again. Janie and Tom and James came to visit, and by the time they left, he was tired and fell asleep. Marcie didn't come to visit again that evening, and Kyle woke in the middle of the night thinking of her.

Was his grandmother right? Was he letting fear dictate his actions? He loved Marcie, and he wanted to protect her and keep her safe. Was that so wrong? On the other hand, if Nana was right, he would be giving up everything he had ever dreamed of. His thoughts chased themselves around and around until he finally fell asleep again, no closer to answers than when he'd woken up.

Ben Jamison came to visit in the morning, and some of Kyle's co-workers came during the day. He enjoyed their visits and looked forward to getting well so he could get back to work. He was beginning to get bored and antsy lying around in the hospital.

Marcie and Betty were visiting him one afternoon when Betty noticed that Kyle seemed to be uncomfortable talking to Marcie. She watched her son carefully and decided it was not just her imagination. He was definitely not the same man who had been so excited at Thanksgiving by the prospect of proposing to Marcie. Betty waited until she was alone with her husband that evening to mention her suspicions.

"I think something is wrong between Kyle and Marcie. At least, there seems to be something on Kyle's part."

Charles Hughes regarded his wife fondly. "What do you mean, dear? Why, just a few weeks ago he was over the moon at the idea of marrying her and starting a new life with her and her children."

"I know, Charles, and that's what has me so worried. He seemed nervous today, and he hardly spoke to her. He couldn't even seem to look her in the eye when she spoke to him. I'm getting worried. It's not like Kyle to avoid facing his problems head-on, and he seemed almost relieved when we left him this afternoon. Maybe you should talk to him."

"Oh, no, I don't think so." He saw that she was going to say something else, and he put his arms around her, drawing her close. "If there is something bothering him, we have to let him work it out for himself. And if there isn't, and I speak to him, it will be really awkward for both of us. If he wants to talk to us, he will. In the meantime, we need to just keep going to visit him and let him and Marcie work things out for themselves."

Betty sighed against her husband's chest. She slipped her arms around him and blinked back the tears that threatened. "Oh, dear, I hope you're right. I'm probably seeing something that isn't there. I just want him to be happy, and I really do like Marcie and her family. I couldn't have picked a woman I'd rather have for a daughter-in-law if I'd tried. She's perfect for him."

"Well, then, let's hope he gets well soon, so they can get married." He chuckled as he set her away from him. "Maybe by next Christmas we'll have another grandchild."

They went down to dinner and didn't mention their conversation to anyone, but both of them noticed that Sallie seemed to be a little quieter than usual. She had spent quite a bit of time alone with Kyle, and Betty and Charles both wondered if she knew something they didn't.

After dinner, they went back into town to visit Kyle. When they got to his room, they saw Marcie, who fled from the room crying. Her face was ashen, her eyes haunted. She didn't stop when they greeted her but ran to the elevator and punched the button to open the doors. She stepped inside, and as the elevator doors closed, they saw her slump against the wall. The three of them stood just outside Kyle's room, looking at one another in shock.

When they went into the room, it was a grim-faced Kyle who sat up in the bed.

"Kyle, what is going on? What on earth happened between you and Marcie?" Betty Hughes hurried to her son's bedside.

He didn't say anything, but held out his hand. As he opened his fist, they saw the engagement ring he had given Marcie. It lay on his palm, the huge emerald looking cold in the dim light.

"I told Marcie I can't marry her." His voice was gruff with tension. "You may as well take this back, Nana."

"Nonsense, my dear. I gave you that ring to give to your fiancée, and I have no intention of taking it back." Sallie Lassiter put her arms around her grandson. "I just wish you had waited and not said anything. I know you think you are doing the right thing, but—"

Betty Hughes interrupted her mother. "Will someone please explain what is going on?"

"I'm sorry, Mom. I guess I should have told you

sooner." Kyle took a steadying breath. "I don't think I can marry Marcie, knowing that I could be shot again and that next time I might not survive. How can I put her through that? I had friends on the force in Dallas whose families lived in dread every day that they wouldn't come home. I went to two funerals while I was on the force and buried two good men I'd worked with. I don't want that to happen to Marcie."

He rubbed a hand across his eyes. "It always seemed safer here than in Dallas, but now I know it could happen here as easily as in any big city."

Charles sat down on the edge of the bed. "Has Marcie ever said anything to make you think she wants you to give up your job?"

"No, Dad, but how can I put her through what I went through when I lost Ella?"

"It's up to you, of course, Kyle, but I think you're selling yourself and Marcie short. You're willing to throw away a chance for love and a family for something that may never happen. We can't live in fear and worry over what might happen someday. That isn't really living." Charles echoed what Kyle's grandmother had told him days earlier.

"I never took you for a coward, son, and I hope you'll really think about this. Marcie is a strong woman, and she loves you. From the look of her when we arrived, I'd say she doesn't agree with you." Charles placed a hand on his son's shoulder and squeezed. "Just don't do this unless you are absolutely sure."

He stood up and took his wife's hand. "Shall we go and let Kyle rest? Think about what I said, Kyle. We'll be back tomorrow."

They said their good nights and left the room. As they stood waiting for the elevator, Betty said, "I hope Marcie made it home all right. We need to go by her house to be sure." They drove by Marcie's and saw her car in the yard but didn't stop to talk to her.

Marcie had cried when Kyle first told her he couldn't marry her, then gotten angry that he had presumed to tell her that he knew what was best for her. How dare he tell her they shouldn't get married because he might be killed in the line of duty? If he didn't want to marry her, she wouldn't beg him to change his mind. He could just rot in that hospital bed before she went to him and begged him to marry her.

Yeah, right, her inner voice taunted. *You're just going to sit here and let him walk away from you? You love him, don't you?*

She barely slept that night, and the lack of sleep showed on her face in the morning. Jane commented on the dark circles under her eyes, asking if she was still worried about Kyle.

"I thought he was recovering nicely. Has there been a change?"

Marcie shook her head. "No, Aunt Jane. He's doing well, and the doctors are pleased by his progress. I just didn't sleep well last night." Marcie tried to keep her hand out of sight so her great-aunt wouldn't notice the missing engagement ring. She managed to get the children off to school and the breakfast dishes cleaned up before Kyle's grandmother came to the house.

Sallie Lassiter accepted a cup of tea, and the three women sat in the kitchen. Sallie broached the subject of the broken engagement, and Jane nearly choked on her tea.

"I'm sorry, Marcie. I didn't realize you hadn't spoken to Jane yet. I just can't believe how stubborn that grandson of mine is." She turned to Jane. "He has decided that if he doesn't marry Marcie, he can protect her from being hurt in case something happens to him. I tried to tell him not to say anything, but apparently he didn't take my advice to heart. He's worried, and after this shooting incident I can see why. But he is also wrong. He's my grandson, and I love him dearly, but he is totally wrong."

She patted Marcie on the hand. "I hope you can forgive him, dear, because he is going to realize he's wrong, and when he does, he is going to need you more than ever."

"I don't know, Sallie. Right now I just don't know. What Kyle did last night hurt, and then, to tell you the truth, it made me angry. I understand about wanting to protect yourself and being afraid to open your heart to love. After what I went through with Jim, I swore I would never fall in love again. And Kyle lost his wife completely unexpectedly to a drunk driver so it must have been even worse for him. But I thought we were so right together, and for the last few months we've spent so much time together. He never once hinted that he was having second thoughts about marrying me."

Chapter Fifteen

Sallie nodded and chose her words carefully before she replied. "He didn't, until he woke up in the ICU. I think the problem is that when Ella was killed, he didn't let himself openly mourn her loss. He thought he needed to be strong for the rest of us, and he tried to bury his heart and his feelings with her. Oh, he's always been kind to Janie and the boys, and he loves his parents and me. But he didn't allow himself to get close to another woman for so long. Then he let himself start to care for someone, and she turned out to be as wrong for him as possible."

The three women drank their tea in silence, thinking about what Sallie had said. It was Jane who finally broke the silence.

"What do you plan to do now, Marcie? Are you going to give up and let the man you love walk away without fighting for him?"

"I don't know how to fight this, Aunt Jane. How do I fight Kyle himself?" Marcie asked.

"Well, not by sitting here moping, that's for sure." Jane stood and smiled at Sallie. "Shall we go sit out on the patio while Marcie gets ready to go to the hospital?" The two older ladies began walking away from Marcie, leaving her sitting at the kitchen table staring after them.

"I can't just go visit him this morning. How can I face him after last night?"

Jane smiled over her shoulder. "I'd suggest a cold cloth on your eyes, and then perhaps just a little makeup to cover the effects of the sleepless night you had. Oh, and wear something green, like that lovely jade-colored silky blouse that brings out the color of your eyes. And get going, for heaven's sake."

Sallie nodded her agreement. "If it was me, I'd walk back into that hospital room and tell him how I felt. I'd tell him we're getting married, and that's all there is to it."

They went out the kitchen door, leaving her alone.

It didn't take long for Marcie to decide that Aunt Jane and Sallie Lassiter were right. She loved Kyle, and she knew he loved her. She would fight for his love, even if it meant doing battle with the very man himself. She was smiling as she put her teacup into the sink.

A short time later Marcie stuck her head out the kitchen door to tell Jane and Sallie she was leaving. They smiled and waved her off, and as soon as she shut the door, they began congratulating each other on the outcome of Sallie's visit.

"Kyle won't know what hit him," that lady confided to her new friend. "They are so obviously right for each other. I have no intention of letting Kyle deprive me of having Marcie and her children in my family."

Jane raised her teacup in a mock salute, and they sat in the sunshine talking as if they had known each other for years instead of weeks.

Kyle was sitting in a chair in his room, his head back and eyes closed. Marcie stood by the door for a moment, looking at the man she loved. She wondered if he was asleep and debated going in and disturbing him. Before she could turn and walk away, though, he opened his eyes.

"Hello, Kyle."

A quick flash of emotion, possibly surprise, was replaced by a guarded look on his face. "Marcie. I didn't think you'd be here today."

She crossed the room and kissed him lightly on the cheek, then sat on the side of his bed. "If you think I'm going to let you run me off, you had better think again, Kyle. I admit, I was stunned last night, and I may have left you with the impression that it was over between us."

He looked at her warily. "I meant what I said, Marcie. I love you too much to put you through this as my wife." He gestured at their surroundings.

"I love you too, Kyle, which is why I'm not going to give you up. I know you think you're being noble, trying to spare me, but I'm a lot stronger than you think." She held up a hand to silence him when he would have interrupted her.

"Please, hear me out. We've talked about so many things in the last few months, I thought we had covered everything. I guess I was wrong. There is one thing we didn't talk about. Your job. I just assumed you would keep your job after we were married. I never for a moment thought about asking you to give it up. Your job is part of who and what you are. It was because of your job that we met."

She paused for a breath, and he wanted to say something, but she rushed on before he could speak.

"Kyle, I love you. I want to be part of your life and to have you in mine. I don't care what you do for a living. I see a lot more than your uniform when I look at you. I see a kind, caring man, a man who tries to help everyone he meets. I see a man who makes me weak in the knees when he kisses me. I see a man who can sit with my children and put puzzles together on the dining room table. My ex-husband would have pitched a fit if the dining room table hadn't been set for dinner every night, even if he didn't bother to come home for it."

She slid off the bed and wrapped her arms around him, careful not to put too much pressure on his wounds, kneeling next to his chair.

"Please don't throw away what we have. I know you tried for years to protect yourself from being hurt after your wife died. But sometimes you just have to take a chance and let yourself trust. I love you, Kyle, and you make me think about things I thought were lost to me forever. I want to share my life with you. To be there for you when you've had a hard day and need someone to talk to. I want to tell you about my day over a cup of tea after the children are in bed. I want to listen as you read to the kids after dinner. I want us to have what my children and I didn't have in my first marriage, and what you weren't able to have with Ella. I want us to be a loving family, committed to each other and to building something for the future."

She leaned her head against his shoulder, and he turned his head so his cheek lay against hers. Neither of them saw his parents in the doorway of the room. Charles and Betty slipped away silently, not wanting to interrupt the tender scene in their son's hospital room.

"What happens if I get shot again?" Kyle asked the question he knew would tear them apart.

Marcie pulled back so she could look into his eyes. "I'll sit by your bedside and tell you how much I love you and pray for your recovery. The same thing I did this time."

"And if I don't survive?"

"Kyle, I don't believe in hiding my head in the sand. I know something could happen. I also don't believe in living my life according to what *might* happen. If I start being afraid of every thing that could occur, I wouldn't be able to get out of bed every day. I am thankful for every day that I am alive, and I take as many precautions as I can to be safe. I use my seat belt when I drive, I don't smoke, and I try to eat right and exercise to stay healthy. I save money for the children's college expenses. I have some plans for our financial future. At the same time, I'm aware that there are things I can't control, and I refuse to let worry over them rule my life." She touched his cheek with her fingertips.

"I love you, Kyle, and I want to spend the rest of my life with you. As far as I'm concerned, a short time together would still be far better than no time together at all. I'm not going to give you up."

For a long moment, time stopped as they stared into each other's eyes. Then he pulled her to him and kissed her with an intensity that they hadn't previously felt. They were both breathless when he broke the kiss.

"I love you too, Marcie." He held her close and

kissed her lightly on the cheek, then trailed kisses along the side of her neck. "I'd like to try to explain something to you, if you'll listen."

She pulled back from him and looked into his eyes. There was something there she couldn't read. "Of course I'll listen."

"You'll probably think I'm crazy, but waking up in the hospital scared me because I really knew at that moment that I could easily die. I wasn't scared for myself but for you. I've just found you, and I had to face the fact that I could be leaving you before we even had a chance to make a life together. I knew I could be leaving you to mourn what might have been."

He looked steadily into her eyes, and what he saw there must have reassured him. "I'm sorry, Marcie. I'm usually not a coward, and I wouldn't blame you if you walked away from me for the way I hurt you last night. I've seen how some women can't handle being a cop's wife, and I've seen how the stress tears families apart. I honestly didn't think about that until I had my experience in the ICU. All this time we've been dating, it never crossed my mind. And then suddenly it was all I could think about."

He pulled her closer, and she slid her arms around him.

"Can you forgive me for hurting you last night? Seeing you run out of here crying tore my heart in half. If you'll forgive me and take back your ring, I promise I'll spend the rest of my life trying to make it up to you."

She turned her face up so he could kiss her, and he obliged very nicely. Once again they were both breathless when the kisses ended.

A discreet cough from the doorway caused them to break apart as the doctor walked into the room.

"Well, Mr. Hughes, I'm glad to see you're feeling better." He was smiling broadly. "Oh, and one more thing. I expect to be invited to the wedding." He made a few notes on Kyle's chart and left the room, chuckling.

"Marcie, look in the drawer of the nightstand," Kyle said. "There's something in there that belongs to you."

She opened the drawer and saw the ring. As she picked it up, the diamonds winked in the light. She held it in her hand and moved back to stand next to Kyle. Holding out her hand to him, she said, "Would you do the honors, Kyle?"

He took the ring from her and slipped it back onto her finger. She leaned down and kissed him lightly on the lips. Drawing back, she smiled and sat down on the edge of his bed.

Before either of them could say anything, a nurse came into the room, followed by a young man who introduced himself as a physical therapist. Realizing she was not going to be able to talk to Kyle alone, Marcie decided to leave. She said good-bye, assuring Kyle she would be back before lunch.

She met his parents in the lobby near the elevator and filled them in on the morning's events. They both hugged her, assuring her that they were thrilled to see her wearing the ring again.

Jane and Sallie echoed that sentiment when Marcie arrived home. She wasn't a bit surprised to find both of them waiting for her when she walked into the house.

Now that Kyle was on the mend, his parents decided to go home the day after Christmas. His grandmother would stay with Andrew and Sharon, who offered her a room for as long as she needed it. She planned to move in with Kyle when he was released and stay with him until he was strong enough to be by himself.

The physical therapist worked with Kyle daily, and it wasn't long before Kyle was badgering the doctor to allow him to go home. The day he was allowed to go home was a joyous occasion. It was a Saturday morning, and it was Christmas Eve.

Marcie, her parents, and her children, Jane, Jack, and Nancy, Tom, Janie, Tom Jr., and James were waiting at his house when his parents and Sallie drove him home from the hospital. The yard was full of balloons, and a huge WELCOME HOME banner hung over the doorway.

Sheriff Jamison, Sarah, and several of the deputies and their families came by to join the welcoming committee. A number of townspeople who knew Kyle also came by to welcome him home and put in a word of appreciation for the way he did his job. When it became apparent that Kyle was getting tired, Sallie insisted he go to bed and rest. Fortunately he lived in a ranch-style house and did not have to climb any stairs.

After just a little good-natured grumbling that Sallie was going to be a hard taskmaster, Kyle consented to taking a nap.

When he woke up, the house was quiet. He lay in bed for a few minutes, thinking about the people who had turned out to welcome him home. He had expected Marcie and her family, and Janie and the boys, Ben Jamison and the others from the sheriff's department, but the others had surprised him. He knew a lot of people in town, and many of them had come by the hospital once he was out of the ICU, but he was a bit surprised at just how many people had come to the house.

It was nice knowing he was appreciated and that he had so many friends. They had gone to a lot of trouble to make his first day home from the hospital special, and he was touched by their efforts.

He rose and got dressed, pulling on sweatpants and a T-shirt. He slowly made his way to the living room. His parents and grandmother were there. He smiled as he eased down onto the couch next to his grandmother.

"Thanks, Nana, for watching out for me." He kissed her on the cheek. "That nap was just what I needed."

They talked about the welcome-home party and the people who had contributed food for it and attended it. The doorbell rang several times, and his mother or father answered it to keep him from having to get up and down. The callers were people who had heard he was home from the hospital and wanted to stop by and drop off food. His fridge and freezer were full of casseroles, salads, pies, and cakes by the time the last caller left.

As they sat at the dinner table, his mother said, "You have wonderful neighbors, Kyle. I won't worry about you so much now that I've seen what the people here have done."

Betty Hughes would still worry about her son. It was something the parent of a law-enforcement officer couldn't help. But knowing there were so many people who cared made the burden lighter. Knowing Marcie Connor was here for him helped even more.

They spent a quiet evening, and finally Kyle had to admit he was tired, even though he had taken that nap earlier.

By eight-thirty, Kyle was ready for bed. He said his good nights and went to his bedroom. He debated calling Marcie. She had had a long day too, and he wasn't sure she would still be up. He lay down and knew he wouldn't sleep until he had talked to her.

Chapter Sixteen

Marcie answered the phone on the third ring. Just hearing her say hello lifted Kyle's spirits.

"Hello, Marcie. I wanted to call and thank you for everything you did to make today happen."

"Hi, Kyle. You're welcome. I was glad to help Sallie. She and Aunt Jane did most of the work. I hope we didn't tire you out too much."

He laughed. "I wouldn't say that, although the nap Nana insisted on sure felt good. I had another reason for calling." He paused to get into a more comfortable position on the bed. "I didn't want to go to sleep without calling and telling you how much I love you. If I'd had my foolish way, we would have been calling off the wedding. Thank you for not giving up on me." He winced as he moved and a twinge of pain reminded him of just how fragile he still was. "This is definitely not how I planned to spend Christmas Eve."

"I love you too, Kyle. And our wedding will take place in the spring, as we planned. By the time the flowers are in bloom, you'll be strong enough to stand in the garden and watch me walk down the aisle."

After they hung up, Kyle lay on his bed in the darkened bedroom, thinking about the miracle that was Marcie. It was a long time before he fell asleep, but he didn't mind. Just thinking about the future with Marcie was comforting.

Christmas dinner was held at Marcie's house. All the members of the two families joined together to celebrate the day. After dinner Kyle settled on the couch in the living room, and the twins climbed up on either side of him. Laurel asked for a story, and he began reading to them from one of the books that had been under the Christmas tree.

Emily sat on the floor, drawing a picture. When the story was finished, Emily showed Kyle the drawing.

Her picture showed a family standing in front of a Christmas tree. The tree stood in front of a bow window that looked very much like the one in Marcie's living room—the one behind Marcie's own Christmas tree, which provided bright splashes of color with its twinkling lights, ornaments, and stacks of gaily wrapped packages. In the picture, a dark-haired man was standing with a red-haired woman and three children who had hair colors just like Seth, Laurel, and Emily.

The people were depicted from the back, looking at the tree. A large circle ran around the five figures, and Kyle studied the drawing for a few minutes, trying to determine the meaning behind the circle. Finally he asked Emily about it, and she quietly said, "It's a circle of love. I wanted us to be in the circle together. You know, if you draw a heart around those you love, well, a heart can be broken. But a circle is forever."

Kyle looked at the child standing in front of him and felt a rush of emotion. He couldn't speak for the overwhelming love he felt for this family. He pulled Emily to him and hugged her, meeting Marcie's eyes over the child's head.

He mouthed the words *I love you* and had to blink back the tears that threatened to fall as he saw the look on her face. It was a humbling experience for him, being accepted into this family without reservation. Feeling the weight of Laurel and Seth cuddled up beside him and having Emily draw him into the family brought home the certainty that what he and Marcie planned was right. He loved these children even if he hadn't fathered them.

He kissed Emily on the top of her head. "Thank

you, Emily. I'm honored to be included in your picture and in your family."

She smiled shyly and settled down on the floor next to his leg and began drawing another picture. He sat staring at the picture in his hands.

"I'm sorry I don't have presents for everyone."

His grandmother heard his comment and said, "Just having you well is all the present we need." Sallie Lassiter smiled at the scene in front of her. Seeing Kyle on the couch surrounded by the children warmed her heart.

"We have presents for you," Seth announced. He slid off the couch and ran to the Christmas tree. He pulled out several of the wrapped packages from beneath the tree. "See? All these are for you, Kyle."

Seth pulled the boxes over to the couch where Kyle sat. He placed the boxes on the couch, then climbed up to sit next to Kyle again. Laurel was sitting on one side of him, Seth on the other. He opened his gifts, feeling like the luckiest man on the face of the earth.

A few hours later, with Laurel snuggled up against him, Kyle knew he was about to fall asleep. Marcie smiled at him and announced it looked like it was nap time for him and the twins. Kyle picked Laurel up and slid her into Marcie's waiting arms. Just before he relinquished Laurel, she woke up and looked at him with sleepy eyes.

"I want Kyle to come tuck me in, Mommy."

The little girl snuggled against her mother's neck but kept her eyes on Kyle.

"May I?" He asked softly. "I'd be glad to carry her upstairs for you."

"I'll carry her up, Kyle, but you're welcome to come and tuck her in." When he looked as if he would have objected, Marcie shook her head. "When you're stronger, I'll let you carry her up to bed as often as you like. For now, though, I think you'd better save your strength. Once we're married, you'll have all the chances in the world to carry these kids around. They'll take advantage of you shamelessly if you let them." She smiled and started up the stairs.

Emily followed, and Kyle and Seth went up the stairs together. Kyle held Seth's hand as the boy walked slowly beside him up the wide stairway.

"They'll make a lovely family, won't they, Jane?" Sallie smiled at her friend. "I hope they don't wait too long to give me more great-grandchildren."

The two older ladies settled down for a cozy chat as they waited for Marcie and Kyle to come back downstairs.

Once the children were settled into bed, Kyle and Marcie stood in the hallway outside the girls' room. He pulled her into his arms and held her close.

"Thank you for sharing your family Christmas with me."

It felt good to stand encircled in his arms. She looked up at him and saw only happiness in his eyes. He dipped his head and brushed his lips against hers, increasing the pressure as she responded to him. He kissed her until she began to feel boneless, unable to stand without his supporting arms, then pulled back, breaking off the kisses.

"We'd better be getting back downstairs. I can't forget that my family is sitting in your living room." He kissed her once more, a quick, hard kiss, then released her.

"I must look a mess," Marcie said. She opened the door into the bathroom that was located between the kids' rooms. A quick peek into the mirror confirmed that her color was high and her hair was mussed from having him tangle his hands in it.

"I do look a mess. They'll know for sure what we've been doing." She picked up a brush and gave her hair a few quick strokes, trying to restore order to it.

"You're beautiful, Marcie, and I think everyone downstairs is smart enough to know I can't resist kissing you." He pulled her by the hand out into the hallway. "And if we don't go now, I'm not going to be able to resist kissing you again." He was laughing as they went down the stairs.

His mother was speaking as they stepped off the stairs. The two families had become firm friends, and Kyle's mother had even expressed an interest in moving to the area. "I hope to have more grand-children to spoil fairly soon, and there's no need for us to be so far away."

Her statement caused Marcie to blush as the assembled members of both families laughed openly.

Kyle ended up taking a nap on the couch while the rest of the families gathered in the kitchen.

Tom Hughes came to Marcie and told her how much he appreciated what Marcie and her father had done for his sons. He had one year left until he could retire from the Navy after twenty years, and he knew how difficult it had been for Janie and the boys, with him gone so much. The boys loved working with Marcie and her family, and Tom was touched by their kindness to his sons. He was grateful that the boys had found something they both enjoyed working at, something that had helped them settle down.

Marcie was more than happy to give the credit for the changes in Tom Jr. and James to her father and brother and to let Tom Hughes know that all the members of her family appreciated how hard the boys were working.

When Kyle came into the kitchen and sat at the table, he looked as if the nap had helped. Shortly after he woke up, the twins and Emily woke from their naps, and the family moved into the playroom to watch a Christmas movie. Several times she caught Kyle looking at her with such a loving expression on his face that it took her breath away. At one point, when no one was looking, he kissed her and murmured, "I love you so much. Let's not wait too long to add to our family once we're married."

He laughed before she could ask him any questions.

"If it's this much fun with three, think how great it will be with a few more. I've been waiting so long for this, I don't want to put off having children."

Later that evening, as they were setting the table for supper, Emily asked her mother if she could speak to her. Marcie sat down at the table and pulled her daughter onto her lap.

"I've been thinking, Mom. Do you think maybe Kyle would mind if I call him 'Dad' after you're married?"

Marcie pulled her daughter to her and hugged her. "I'm sure Kyle would be thrilled, Emily. Why don't you ask him after supper?"

She wanted to ask why Emily wanted to call Kyle "Dad" but wasn't sure exactly how to phrase the question. She didn't have to figure it out, though, as Emily continued.

"All my friends talk about their fathers, and I wish I had a father to do stuff with. When we went bowling that time, they all thought he was so cool." She paused. "When he's here, he always helps us with our homework and puts puzzles together with us. And he never yells at us. She hugged her mother and then whispered, "I love him too, Mom. I didn't want to like him 'cause I thought he just wanted to take you away from us, but he doesn't mind having us around. Like when he plays games with us or reads to us. He's nice to us even when you aren't around."

"I think Kyle will be very glad to have you call him 'Dad,' sweetheart. I know how much he loves you." Marcie was proud of her daughter and the way she had changed her mind about Kyle. She was certain they would be happy when they were living together as a family.

When Emily asked him after supper that night if she could call him "Dad," Kyle felt honored. This was truly a wonderful Christmas, and he knew he would remember it always.

He also considered himself fortunate that he hadn't managed to drive Marcie away during the first few days after he was shot. He was lucky to have her, and he intended to tell her so every day for the rest of their lives.

He was waiting for her at the bottom of the stairs when she came down after putting the children to bed. They were alone for the first time all day. The only illumination came from the lights strung on the Christmas tree.

He held out his arms, and she stepped into them. There was no need for words as his mouth sought hers in a searing kiss. She kissed him back without reservation, and neither of them noticed the three children who crept quietly to the top of the stairs, saw them kissing, and ran giggling and smiling to their bedrooms.

Epilogue

On the first Saturday in May, Marcie and Kyle said their vows at Harmony Farm. It was a beautiful, sunny afternoon, and the gardens were in bloom.

Kyle stood by the gazebo, surrounded by their families and friends. He watched Emily and Laurel walk toward him, scattering flower petals. Seth stood next to him, having walked down the aisle first, holding the pillow with the rings on it. His brother, Tom, stood on his other side, acting as best man. Kyle waited as Marcie began to walk toward him on the arm of her father.

As she walked down the aisle, Marcie looked beautiful in an ivory-colored gown. She wore a short veil and carried a bouquet of pink and ivory roses, sweet peas, and peonies.

181

Marcie moved to stand next to Kyle, her eyes on his. He looked so handsome in his tuxedo. Her father stood next to her until the minister asked, "Who gives this woman in marriage?" Andrew Greer answered the minister, kissed Marcie's cheek, and stepped back to sit next to his wife.

When the minister pronounced them husband and wife, Kyle took Marcie into his arms, lifted her veil, and kissed her gently.

Everyone who witnessed the marriage knew that today, in this garden setting, love was truly in bloom.